THE EMBER WAR SERIES
BOOK 2

Cover by The Illustrated Author Design Services.

Contact Leia@LeiaStone.com for Business inquiries

LUSKA
THE WALL

THUNDER CLIFF

SKY REACH

EVERGREEN
GOLDEN HILLS
CEDAR CREEK
AMERSEA

MARBLE SHORES
RIVERINE
THE COVE

STORM HAVEN

Imbria
The Wilds

BOOK ONE RECAP

DO NOT READ UNLESS YOU WANT 100% SPOILERS.

In book one, *Lies that Bleed,* Aisling Everhart, the emperor's daughter, catches her boyfriend Jace cheating the morning of the Lottery but vows not to cry over it. After Tetra, her best friend who suffers from a life-long leg injury, gets picked in the Lottery to enter the Wilds, Aisling is worried she will be killed. Her father's sworn enemy, Kohen Badshah, offers an alliance to keep Tetra alive. Aisling agrees only if *he* isn't in the alliance. She can't be seen with him. He's an Imbrian, and Amersea took over his country after the Great Blackout, where his father was declared a terrorist and killed.

Once in the Wilds, Aisling has to protect Tetra and Kohen's "family". The group of Imbrians is in a fragile truce, and Aisling butts heads with Anika but ends up liking her snarky attitude.

On the first night, Kohen is nearly killed by Aisling's father's men, and without thinking, Aisling runs into the woods and saves his life... killing two imperial soldiers to do so. She's horrified, unsure why she would do such a thing, but also thinks that maybe Kohen isn't the monster her father warned her about.

Aisling is relieved when Tetra safely bonds a wolf creature named Ariel. But when both she and Kohen get to day three, they are desperate for a bonding. Aisling follows Kohen into the Wilds out of suspicion to find that he's actually hunting Talanagi. She thinks he's insane but follows him down river, around the Wall, and into the rival nation of Luska. There, Kohen bonds a black dragon named Onyx, and she bonds a firebird named Liana.

In bonding her bird, she is burned alive and dies.

Aisling wakes up three days later in a body bag... reborn. The coroner is horrified by this newfound gift and calls her father, the emperor. Aisling is terrified her dad will see her ability to escape death as a threat to him, but he's mostly happy Aisling is alive and has bonded Liana.

The night before boot camp, Aisling goes to a club to find out that Kohen knows where her creature is. Liana has been missing since Aisling died. Someone has been keeping Liana from rebirthing so that Aisling can't finish their bond. With Kohen's help, she frees Liana and seals their bond.

Once they enroll in boot camp, Aisling is quickly taken aback by Kohen's genuine gestures: he secures her mother's necklace so it won't be confiscated; he gets mad at Jace for stealing her food and they fight over it. He's protective of her, which pleases her and pisses her off at the same time.

It's not until a mock attack on the campus that Aisling learns someone is out to kill her. Kohen stops her from confronting the drill sergeant, who she overheard plotting her demise, saying she needs to be searching for the bigger boss who sent down the orders. She's suspicious of Kohen. Her father killed his. He could be playing nice with her just to get her to trust him so he can then kill her...

But that doesn't happen. She learns Kohen has an incredible gift, the gift of seeing the future. This type of power will get you killed in Amersea, and so she swears not to tell a soul. Kohen is tortured by his future visions with Aisling. He sees them in love, together, and here she is dancing with Alek. He can't handle it, and she doesn't know what to do. He tells her of a future attack on the campus, and she isn't sure what to make of it.

Admiral Blade and his creature, Sahiri, are about to force Kohen and Aisling to show their powers in front of everyone. That would get Kohen killed and maybe even Aisling if she burst into flames and was reborn. The admiral grips Aisling's jaw when she refuses to allow Sahiri to display her power, and Kohen attacks the admiral. They are jailed and interrogated by Admiral Caruso, who has the ability to ferret out lies, and then they are let free. Aisling is able to dance around the truth and not let Kohen's secret out.

During another mock campus drill and another attempt on Aisling's life, a new, terrifying power emerges in her: the thrall. She can control minds. It is a gift that Liana says her very own grandmother had. It's dangerous, and if anyone were to find out, they would kill Aisling. It seems both she and Kohen have secrets that need keeping.

Aisling waits for Kohen to betray her, but he's loyal, protective, and clearly into her. So at the graduation night party, when she hears her cheater ex-boyfriend Jace talking crap about her and Kohen stands up for her, she walks in the room and kisses him in front of everyone. It's good to see Jace's face of shock, but she regrets hurting Alek, who saw the kiss and has had a thing for her.

She leaves the room to go in search of Tetra, when Kohen finds her again and tells her of a new vision. There is an attack on the training center happening right now, and someone she loves will die.

She decides the only way to warn her father of the attack without getting Kohen killed is to tell her father that she has Kohen's gift of future sight. Her father believes her, making a portal to the training center to warn everyone.

When Kohen and Aisling get to the training center, it's already a war zone. They fight a blonde Luskin female on a red dragon with the ability to steal breath. Aisling is forced to use her power in front of the red dragon rider in order to save her own life. Now the red rider knows Aisling can control minds. The red dragon rider gets away, but Liana and Aisling defeat the Luskins and win the battle.

But not without cost.

Nikhil dies trying to protect Anika, and Aisling worries for a moment that Tetra is the one close to her that will perish, as Kohen predicted. But her best friend is unharmed and even demonstrates a great ability to shield.

She is just thinking that Kohen was wrong when Admiral Caruso comes out and informs her that her father is dead and she needs to be sworn in as empress immediately.

Aisling runs to see her father's dead body, falling into sobs as Kohen holds her. Someone has killed him. There are no apparent marks at first to indicate how such a strong man would die.

The book ends with Aisling declaring that whoever has made her and her sisters orphans will meet death.

CHAPTER ONE

I stared down at my father's corpse with a lump in my throat. He was pale, with sickly blue veins scattered across his face. His lips were tinged purple. Despite coroner Davis' efforts to make him look presentable with makeup, he looked... dead.

Because he was.

My father is dead. The emperor is dead.

"We are waiting for the blood results, but we think it was some kind of poison, as no other wounds were found on his body but those claw marks."

I knew the marks he spoke of, the ones on my father's arms that were currently hidden under the sheet. I'd seen them on him the night he was killed. Last night. How had it only been last night? It felt like years and only seconds at the same time.

"Poisoned claws? Talons?" I asked, dragging my gaze away from my father's face for the first time.

"We think so," Davis said. "There was no evidence of a toxin in his stomach, so he didn't drink it. The test results will show more."

I nodded. That was good. Drinking the poison meant it would have been one of our own who had close contact with him. I didn't even want to go there. But there had been foam on his lips—did Davis see that? It was gone now. Did it matter? My mind was racing and sluggish at the same time as I tried to process too much at once.

Admiral Caruso, who stood next to me, turned to face me. "Are you ready, Empress?"

I was sworn in late last night, a mere six minutes after my father was found dead. The city was now secured, so I sent for Elaine and my sisters to be escorted back to Riverine with a personal guard of over a dozen imperial soldiers. They would be here any moment. I was about to fly across the country with the morning sun and parade myself to my people as a strong and capable woman. As their empress.

I tipped my chin high, pushing down every emotion I wanted to feel right now, closing it off, and forcing myself to be numb to the wild mixture of pain and rage that was threatening to drown me.

I nodded. "Yes, Admiral."

I then looked at Davis. "The second you have any lead on

what type of poison this was, I want a full report. I don't care about the hour of the night."

He saluted me. "Yes, Empress."

I would find the person who killed my father and cleave their head from their shoulders with his sword that now hung on my hip.

I hadn't slept. I hadn't eaten. Everything was happening so quickly, but I had to push through. I had to stay strong. It's what my father would have expected, what my people demanded of me.

When we stepped out of the morgue, I stopped in my tracks, the ball in my throat growing tighter. The Riverine flag that hung over Emberlane Park was half-mast.

I would be the first to admit that my father wasn't a warm person. He didn't kiss our boo-boos when younger or bounce us on his knee. But he loved us in other ways, *better ways,* some might say. He taught me battle strategy over breakfast at fourteen.

'Sometimes you have to make your opponent think you are weak so that you can draw them closer.' I remembered all of his advice—I'd cataloged it for the day I would lead. A day I thought would be decades in the future. *'Then you go for their throat.'*

My father's love was shown in the way he'd hired Elaine to train me and my sisters. He'd bought us weapons and taught us how to use them. He kept us safe. He...

I turned off the thoughts as a line of admirals and their

creatures stepped out of the waiting caravan of black cars. Liana descended from the sky to take me on my tour of the countryside.

Admiral Caruso faced me with her tawny wolf creature at her side and pulled a stiff salute to her forehead. "The empire is looking to you now, Empress Aisling," she counseled. "To lead without fear. To get retribution for this travesty. Show them how strong the Everhart name is."

I nodded.

A shadow passed overhead. Liana landed beside me, and the admiral took a wary step back, eyeing her with apprehension.

Liana peered over at me. *'Elaine and your sisters are down the street. Do you want to wait for them or see them after the parade?'*

I'd sent a messenger with a protection team early this morning to deliver the news of our father's death to them. I wasn't sure I could face my sisters and Elaine now and still fly around the empire and remain strong.

'Let's go. I'll see them later,' I said, and adjusted my black leather armor before hopping onto her back, careful with the yellow cast I still wore on my wrist.

Without questioning, she took to the skies, and my anxiety eased once we were among the clouds. I was exhausted, hungry, sad, confused, enraged. So many emotions ran through me, but when Liana came up over Emberlane Park and thousands of Riverine citizens erupted into applause, I pushed all of my desires down and focused on the needs of my people.

A full smile would not be appropriate as I was still mourning my father, so I opted instead for a tight, barely there smile and a constant slow wave. Liana flew circles above the people as children held up signs with my firebird creature painted on them.

"Long live Empress Aisling!" the crowd chanted.

I pulled my father's sword from my belt and hefted it into the sky, and the cheers grew louder. This was a promise of retribution for the attack last night. I would hammer the Luskins hard and long for what they did. Already, the leaders of the Fleet were drawing up battle plans to present to me tonight after my tour. Together, we would seek the best course of action that would incur minimal losses on our side and maximum loss on Luska's.

After about ten minutes at the park, Liana moved on to the hillside mansions. Citizens waved from their backyards and porches, all looking to the sky as if waiting for me. Every flag in the city was half-mast. It was a weird tradition we had in Amersea. We didn't truly mourn a fallen emperor or empress. That was seen as a sign of weakness. There would be no funeral for my father, no throngs of black and weeping eyes. Instead, we lowered our flags for a day and then looked to the future and strength of our country. We lifted up the successor and trudged on. My father's nice suit and painted face were merely for me and Elaine and the triplets. Once they said goodbye to him, he would be cremated in accordance with his wishes.

'Who do you think killed him?' I asked Liana as we flew over a stretch of barren forest on our way to the first Fleet base in our tour, Storm Haven.

'Poison not ingested means it was not likely anyone in Amersea double-crossing him. I think one of the Luskins' creatures had deadly poisoned talons and must have snuck in and attacked him during the assault.'

I nodded. It was a good assessment; the same one I had come to, and yet... something else felt off about how my father died. He was so strong. Zuri too. For him to fall so easily... it was hard for me to believe. That room should have been covered in blood; my father would have been missing an arm or leg before someone killed him. He would have likely just portaled out in extreme danger. My father was not immortal, but I had expected his killer's body to be lying next to him at least. He had no blood under his nails or on his blade. He was taken by surprise and barely fought back. It didn't seem possible.

'You think Red could have taken the air from his lungs from afar?' I asked Liana, indicating the woman who rode the red dragon. She had a dangerous power I'd never encountered before.

'Yes, but then his lips would have been blue, right?' Liana said wisely.

She was right. His lips were purple now, but they hadn't

been on the night he died. He'd not looked like he lacked oxygen. Maybe it didn't matter exactly who killed him or how. I was going to strike back on Luska in my father's name either way.

Liana cocked her head to the side, and I felt her body tighten beneath me.

'What is it?'

She relaxed. *'Onyx and Kohen are flying far behind us, out of sight. Kohen is worried about your safety.'*

Kohen. The name brought an ache to my chest. Just when I thought I might be able to have a nice little love affair with him before any real responsibility was laid at my feet, my father died and made me empress. Anything I'd started with Kohen would have to stop now.

My people would never follow a leader tied to an enemy.

I sighed.

Was Kohen right to be worried about my safety? Would whoever killed my father come back to finish me off and then my sisters? With thoughts like that, I'd never sleep again, so I pushed them down.

Admiral Caruso and some other high-level Imperial Fleet members were following my parade by road and train. If they knew that Kohen Badshah was following me, they'd probably lock him up and kill him. We trusted no one right now.

'Tell him to go home,' I told Liana.

I didn't want to deal with Kohen right now. Or Tetra, or

anyone else. I had way too much on my plate to be thinking of my friends. I was now the leader of the entire Imperial Fleet, the entire nation of Amersea. At nineteen years old.

'He said he will stay out of sight but he's not leaving,' Liana answered.

I growled but didn't have the mental space to care if Kohen wanted to follow me across the country. I let my thoughts wander to the night Kohen told me I was going to lose someone I loved. He'd said he didn't know at the time who it was, but now I wondered if he'd foreseen it was my father and didn't tell me. Before I could think more on it, Liana descended into Storm Haven base, where rows and rows of imperial soldiers stood waiting, standing with stiff backs and firm salutes.

One by one, the soldiers broke protocol and peered up at the sky to watch me descend. My father's parade had been by car. Never had an emperor or empress *flown* on her parade. But we thought it would be a good show of strength. The admirals wanted the people of Amersea to know that their new empress was bonded to a Talanagi.

I landed in the middle of the seaside base that perched on the cliff of the beautiful ocean. I couldn't help but think of how my father wanted to send me here. And now I'd be going to Sky Reach to live on the front. I'd gotten my wish in the worst way. I didn't have the power to portal home every night for dinner like my father.

I dismounted Liana, and she stood tall, peering at the

soldiers as I walked toward where a podium had been erected. I knew some type of a speech would be expected of me, no matter how small, but I hadn't taken speech-writing training yet, so I'd have to wing it.

I glanced out at the rows of creatures who stood off to the side, waiting for their bondeds. Lions, wolves, bears, tigers, foxes, falcons, gorillas, formidable beasts waiting for *my* command.

Beside the podium was the general of the base. I couldn't remember his name, and I knew I'd have to sit down with flashcards after today and memorize every single officer in the Fleet, but for now, I just nodded to him.

He saluted me. "Empress."

"General." I tipped my head, trying to swallow my nerves.

He gestured to the stage as if asking me to give my speech, and my palms went slick with sweat. I hated public speaking, but it was part of this new life, so I glanced at Liana for reassurance, and she gave me a small nod. I stepped up to the podium and surveyed the mass of soldiers before me. Each one was a valuable life that was now in my hands.

With no plan, I leaned into the microphone and told the soldiers of Storm Haven the truth: "My father, your fallen emperor, was murdered last night during the Luskin attack on Riverine."

Each soldier present removed their hand from their

salute and crossed it over their heart. A gesture of respect for my father that had my throat tightening.

"But I am here to tell you that the streets of Luska will run red with the blood of their soldiers because I will not sleep until I have paid them back in kind!" I screamed, my voice rising with each word.

The soldiers shouted their agreement, throwing their fists into the air. "And this war cannot be won without Storm Haven. This base is essential to our efforts. You keep the Imperial Fleet stocked and fed. Without you, we are weak. Don't let anyone diminish your importance."

More cheers, and then I crossed my fist over my chest. "I have trained my whole life to take up this title. I promise to lead you fiercely and wisely until my dying breath." The screaming was roaring in my ears as I stepped off the podium.

The general shook my hand, appearing impressed. "That will boost morale for months to come. Thank you, Empress. We look forward to your orders of retaliation on the Luskins."

I met his gaze with a fiery one of my own. "Oh, you can count on it, General," I told him.

I walked over to Liana, slid my leg over her back, and we took to the skies, heading for the next stop. The soldiers below chanted my name, and I couldn't help the swell of pride that rose in me.

'That was a good speech. You will make a wonderful empress,' Liana told me.

I thanked her and settled into the ride.

WE STOPPED off at Marble Shores, Thunder Cliff, and were now on our way to Evergreen base. After that, I just had Sky Reach. As we passed over Evergreen, I felt dizzy with exhaustion and hunger. It was past lunchtime, and I'd skipped breakfast. I'd been riding for five or six hours straight, and my legs were nearly numb. It was heartwarming to see that even the small country villages came out and looked to the skies to wave at me. I waved back, no matter how tired I was, and sometimes Liana spit fire to give them a show.

When I touched down at Evergreen, I stiffly slid off of Liana.

'I'm going to hunt. I'll be back soon,' she told me as the line of soldiers looked my way.

I saluted them, gave a variation of the same speech I'd given Thunder Cliff and the other bases, and then followed Admiral Caruso to the mess hall. It was jam-packed with soldiers, but they gave us a wide berth. Caruso walked right to the front of the line as I followed with four guards flanking my left and right. I was beyond starving. I felt lightheaded and out of it, and I kicked myself for skipping breakfast and not having even a snack.

The admiral placed food on a tray for herself and then made one of her assistants make a tray for me. She led us to a table in the back, where a line of soldiers stood guard to keep anyone from sitting. It was weird to be segregated like this, but I'd have to get used to it. Being empress meant I was different now, no matter how much I didn't want to be.

I tried to give a nod or small half-smile to everyone we passed, including the eating soldiers. My father only wanted to be feared, but I wanted to be a liked empress. I guess I wanted both. With fear came some amount of respect, but I wanted to be liked, too.

The guards parted like a curtain, and then I sat down across from Admiral Caruso. Her assistant set my food tray before me, and I wondered if I would ever be allowed to carry my own food again. Was it seen as beneath my station? I hadn't ever seen my father cook for himself or do any menial task. *There are people for that*, he would say. I picked up my fork and stabbed a giant potato, holding it to my lips, about to take a bite, when a familiar voice shouted behind me.

"Aisling Everhart, drop it!"

I froze, eyes wide as I spun to see Elaine. Her cheeks were flushed, a few chunks of hair had sprung free of her bun, and her gaze took me in like a mother scanning her child for injuries. A lump formed in my throat. Vespa stood at her side, watching me with a cocked head.

The guards looked back at me and I nodded that they both be allowed in.

"What are you doing here?" I asked her. The guards broke apart, and she approached me. She was wearing her Imperial Fleet uniform, complete with her lieutenant pin. I hadn't seen her in that uniform in a decade. How the hell had she gone from Riverine to Evergreen? She must have taken a train. Where were my sisters? I had so many questions.

Elaine peered from me to Admiral Caruso. "Did you have anyone taste her food?"

I glanced back at the admiral, who appeared confused. I knew the two were friends from their time in the Fleet, but there was an air of tension between them now. Elaine walked over to me and yanked the plate out from under me. Leaning forward, she got right in Admiral Caruso's face. "Did. You. Taste. Her. Food?"

Understanding dawned on the admiral's face. "There was no poison found in her father's stomach. I highly doubt—"

Elaine simply growled, cutting her off.

"Don't forget your rank, Lieutenant Steele. I'm your superior," the admiral warned my governess.

It took me a minute to remember that Elaine's last name was Steele. I hadn't heard her referred to like that in forever.

Elaine scoffed at that. "It was your job to keep the emperor alive. And it's been my job for nineteen years to keep Aisling alive. Who's doing better at their job?"

Ouch.

I winced at Elaine's sharp rebuke. I knew she would take my father's death badly, but this was pretty bad.

Admiral Caruso stood, toe to toe with Elaine. The admiral's wolf creature began to circle Vespa, and I really just wanted to shovel potatoes and chicken into my mouth, but instead, I stood as well. This was one of many scenarios I was sure I would find myself in where I needed to de-escalate. Elaine, ironically, taught me all the de-escalation scenarios.

"Lieutenant Steele." I wasn't sure what was with the uniform—she hadn't been active in the Fleet in forever—but I was going to assume she was wearing it for a reason, so I'd refer to her as such. "You were smart to think of my meal being poisoned. Can we get someone to taste it so I can eat before I start gnawing on my own arm?"

That caused the corner of her lips to quirk into a smile and she reached down and shoved a chunk of potato from my plate into her mouth and began to chew without taking her eyes off of Caruso. I didn't mean *her*! If anything happened to that woman, I would never forgive myself.

In exasperation, I faced Admiral Caruso. "Forgive Lieutenant Steele for overstepping, but like she said, she's kept me alive and trained me for this very job my entire life. I trust her more than I trust any of you."

Hurt flashed across the admiral's face, but she swallowed hard and nodded. The point had been taken. If Elaine wanted extra steps taken to ensure my safety, I wanted that respected.

Elaine ripped off a hunk of chicken and then popped a candied green bean in her mouth, chewing as she stared down the admiral.

Caruso finally rolled her eyes and sat down, breaking the stare. "Okay, Lieutenant, you are right. I should assume all assassination attempts are going to be coming at our new empress. I'll interview food tasters this week—"

"No," Elaine said, sitting as well and seemingly forgetting their tense argument now that she'd won. "I don't trust anyone. I'll do it."

I sat down and faced her. "No way. I need you alive."

Elaine turned to me, and there was so much pain in her eyes. We hadn't talked about my father's death, about me being sworn in, about anything.

"And I need *you* alive, Empress." Her voice shook.

The word *empress* on her lips held so much more meaning. She'd literally educated me my entire life for this. I swallowed multiple times to try to dislodge the lump in my throat. Her hand squeezed mine under the table, and I squeezed back. It was probably the most emotion we would show over this whole thing.

"Fine," I told her. "For now." She let go of my hand and nodded.

Elaine looked under our table. "Has this area been scanned for explosives?"

"Of course it has! I'm not an idiot," Admiral Caruso admonished.

"That's debatable," Elaine said, but there was a smirk on her lips.

The admiral shook her head, smiling a little too now. "What's up with the uniform, Elaine?" She used her first name. I knew the two were close, but not sure *how* close. Being on a first-name basis was rare in the Fleet.

"The second I got back to Riverine with the triplets, I reenlisted and followed Aisling's flyover to here," she told us.

"You what?" I screeched. "Where are my sisters?" She was supposed to train them to be my replacement and keep them safe. How could she do that if she was back in the Fleet?

"They're safe. I stashed them away where no one would think to look—at Tetra's house. I will start interviewing a replacement for my position tomorrow," she said in a low voice only Admiral Caruso and I could hear.

Replace Elaine? Impossible.

"But... they need you." She was the only mother figure we had.

"You need me more, and I won't have close access to you as a civilian," Elaine said.

It took every ounce of self-control I had not to cry right then. Even now she was protecting me like she always had. She'd been inactive for so long, but I never really saw her as a civilian. She was right, though—she wouldn't have clearance to join me in meetings or on base without being a soldier.

"I'm starving. When can I eat?" I asked her, resting my cast on the edge of the table. I wondered when I could take this thing off. It didn't hurt anymore, but I didn't want it to heal wrong.

She consulted her watch. "Two more minutes. Get used to cold food."

I groaned. Over the next half hour, Elaine and Admiral Caruso talked about safety plans for my life going forward. The admiral got annoyed when Elaine found holes in her ideas. In the end, it was decided that the home I had grown up in was now a giant target. Everyone knew we lived there, and now that attacks on Riverine were possible, my sisters and I would be moving to a new, more modest home in an undisclosed location that only a handful of people would know about. The emperor's home would still be a base of operations for meetings and some training for my sisters, but we would not sleep there.

The chicken and potatoes were cold, but no one died eating them, so I wasn't going to complain about dinner. After finishing the food, I bid Elaine and Caruso farewell and told them I would meet them at the next stop before jumping on Liana and taking to the skies.

My last stop was the one I was dreading the most: Sky Reach. It was the most formidable of all the bases we had, and in control of it on a day-to-day basis was Jace's father, Commander Ledger.

Sky Reach was now where I would be posted. My father

used to travel there daily because he had the ability to create portals, but I would now have to live there, visiting Riverine and my sisters on weekends and the occasional holiday. To make things more awkward, I was the empress of the entire nation and leader of the Imperial Fleet, but I would still be undergoing training. I was skilled, but not yet at the level of these men and women. I'd never seen real battle. So they would have to train me by day and take my orders at night. Orders that would be given to me by a council of over a dozen hardened military leaders and advisors.

When Liana began her descent over the notorious base, nervousness flushed through my system, strong and fast. Sky Reach was where the baddest baddies in my father's fleet—my fleet—went to serve. They took the most hits and delivered the worst blows to the Luska side.

I scanned the rows and rows of soldiers lined up in their wrinkle-free uniforms, stiff-backed and eyes forward. The lumps of dirt in the distance indicated underground bunkers, something Sky Reach was known for. Hundreds of creatures all lurked off to the side, standing as stiffly as their bonded in neat, coordinated rows.

Liana landed and not one head turned in my direction. These soldiers were well-trained.

"Empress." Lead Commander Aldric Ledger saluted me as his tiger creature stood erect at his side. Hiro's white fur was streaked with red ember marks. The tiger looked powerful and majestic as he peered up at me. He imbued the commander with extreme strength, enough to tear a man in half without breaking a sweat. I looked up at the sharp lines of the commander's face, and my heart pinched a little. He looked so much like Jace, but Jace felt like a lifetime ago, and I'd made my peace with that betrayal.

"Commander Ledger," I said, which was so weird because I grew up calling him Aldric. I saluted him back, remarking on the fact that I'd had dinner with him and his wife a hundred times. And in that moment, I was reminded of Jace's admission that his parents were getting divorced. It shocked me now to even think of it. They were perfect, or had been, but nothing was perfect anymore.

"I'm sorry to hear about your father," he said.

I nodded my thanks but was spared small talk when Elaine and Admiral Caruso exited the car they'd just rolled in on. Liana had been forced to fly slowly along the roads to keep pace with them at Elaine's insistence. Otherwise, we would have been here in half the time.

"I look forward to this war meeting so that we can pay back these iceheads for what they've done," Commander Ledger growled as Elaine and Caruso walked up.

"Me too," I told him as Elaine and Caruso gave a small salute by way of greeting.

The commander was my father's most trusted advisor. I knew that I would be expected to take his advice. I glanced around. "Where is the podium?" I asked.

The commander peered down at me from his towering

height. "My troops don't need some mushy speech. They need orders. When are we hitting the Luskins back?"

"Shall we just start the meeting, then?" Admiral Caruso asked. "I'm sure you are brimming with ideas."

The commander nodded and moved to lead us back to a black brick building in the center of the base.

They didn't need a speech, he'd said, but I didn't want someone to just take orders from me without knowing why. I didn't want them blindly following me just because I was my father's daughter. The troops stood still in their rows, facing forward, their creatures off to the side as if awaiting instruction. I walked over to a park bench that was sitting off to the side. The metal scraped against the crushed rock as I pulled it over to the front of the troops, facing them head-on.

Admiral Caruso, Elaine, and the lead commander all halted their journey to the brick building in the center of the base as they looked at me expectantly. I leaped up onto the bench and faced my Imperial Fleet.

"Sky Reach!" I bellowed, having no microphone. "*You* are the heart of the Imperial Fleet!" I let my words of praise wash over them and noticed how some of them stood a little taller, watching me in anticipation. I could show no weakness to these men, lest I lose their respect. "You are the crown jewel and the greatest weapon we have. I will need you in the days to come as I plot my revenge on the Luskins for what they've taken from us. For attacking our peaceful capital of Riverine, for the murder of my father, your emperor!" I screamed the last bit until my voice was raw.

The soldiers chanted then, *Ha-rooh, Ha-rooh, Ha-rooh*. It was a call to arms, something only the Sky Reach soldiers did.

"I grew up playing in Emberlane Park in Riverine. I've fished in the streams of Cedar Creek. I've collected shells at Marble Shores and hiked the Golden Hills! This land is my land, *your* land. We have to decide now what we want to leave for future generations. Will we pass down this war to them, or will we conquer Luska for once and for all and end this?!"

The response was deafening. The soldiers broke rank, throwing their fists into the air and screaming so loud that spittle flew from their mouths. They were bloodthirsty, which is exactly how I wanted them. It was exactly how I wanted to set them loose on our enemies.

I stepped off the bench and walked over to where the commander, admiral, and Elaine were waiting for me. The commander appeared slightly annoyed that I'd given the speech, and I knew that with my father gone, he might treat me like some young juvenile who didn't know what they were doing. We'd have to work that out. The soldiers were still chanting when I reached him. "Looks like they do enjoy a good speech after all," I told him.

His nostrils flared, but he nodded. "Looks like they do."

He led Caruso away, but I hung back with Elaine.

"I'll have to take speech-writing lessons. I have no idea what I'm doing," I told her.

Her eyes looked misty as she gave me a crooked smile. "Oh, Aisling, you don't need speech lessons. You know *exactly* what you are doing. I'm proud of you, and your father would be too."

The compliment caught me off guard. Elaine always had some tidbit of advice; nothing was ever perfect for her. We could always improve.

With that, she led me across the courtyard to the famed brick building. A sign stood on a metal pole out front.

"*Command Center: War Room. Approved personal only,*" it read. To the right of the building were a half dozen creatures, probably too large to fit in the room. A lion, an elephant, two wolves, a coyote, and I recognized Admiral Blade's gorilla, Sahiri.

Only when I stepped inside did the chanting of the soldiers outside finally fade. I took stock of the command center and war room, my palms tingling with excitement. I'd only ever glanced in here. My father had intended, of course, to take me to meetings, but on our last visit, he'd said we were short on time, so I'd never officially joined one. The walls were covered in maps, and each map had colored pins or areas circled with notes. On the back wall were two phones and over a dozen handheld radios that squawked with constant information. Over a dozen advisors, ranging from generals to admirals, all stood around a large oak table, and the entire space smelled of coffee. I followed the smell to the pot brewing in the corner. A half dozen creatures stood near their bonded, while those in the room who stood without bonded were probably the ones I had seen outside.

'I'm out here if you need me,' Liana said as if reading my mind.

"Empress." One of the generals turned and saluted me as the rest followed.

This was it. My first war room meeting. My father used to spend hours here with Jace's dad, planning what the next move in the war would be. Then he'd come home and tell me over dinner about the different battle strategies our fleet used and why. I'd literally been training for this my entire life, and yet I felt so small and wildly out of place at that moment. I felt like an imposter. The only reason I stood here was because I was born of my father's bloodline. That was it.

"What is a lieutenant doing here?" Admiral Mirza asked as he eyed Elaine's rank pin.

Elaine opened her mouth to speak, but I beat her to it.

"She's my most trusted advisor," I told him, daring him with my gaze to fight me on this. My father told me that one day, when I took over for him, I'd have to push to gain the respect he had. That his men wouldn't follow anyone weak.

The admiral cleared his throat but nodded.

I approached the table. "I'm eager to listen to all of your ideas on how we can make the Luskins pay after what they did in Riverine, so let's hear it."

The large oak table looked like it had seen hundreds of hours of battle itself. It was covered in knicks, scratches, and coffee cup rings, but I felt so honored to stand over it. It came to about waist high, with no chairs, and right now it was covered with maps of Luska and figurines that signified their army and bases.

Three hours, dinner, and two cups of coffee later, I'd heard every idea. I listened with rapt attention and head nods, giving my opinion and hearing theirs. My team of advisor's best idea was something they had argued over for nearly an hour. It involved sending in a lethal team of a dozen assassins via a ground assault to plant explosives at the Red Palace in Luska Square. But I nixed it because there was no way a dozen men with a dozen creatures were getting clear into the capital without getting caught, tortured, and eventually killed. There was a reason we hadn't tried that before. I didn't want to lose men just for the sake of trying something new. The Luskins would hang their bodies on the Wall to humiliate us. No, it needed to be a plan we could execute perfectly.

"We could poison the river. It flows that way, and we would warn Imbria not to drink from it or bathe—"

I cut Commander Ledger off. "No way. That would kill innocent civilians. Luskin children play in the river. We abide by the War Code even when Luska does not," I warned.

Rule number one: No killing civilians on purpose.

I had never faulted Luskin citizens for their war-thirsty rulers.

The commander glared at me. "Luskin children who will grow up to be Luskin soldiers."

I nodded. "And *then* we will kill them, but not a moment before."

I wasn't sure what kind of ship my father had been running, but poisoning children wasn't going to happen under my rule.

"There has to be another plan," I said, starting to feel my mind fraying at the edges. How long ago did I see my father's dead body lie in the morgue with purple lips? Was that just this morning? It felt like ages ago. I hadn't slept in what felt like years, and I still had to see my sisters and name a successor and—

"We need to go back to the idea of sending in an elite team," the commander said. "A dozen of my best men. They know the consequences. They are willing to die for revenge." Many of his generals grunted their agreement.

I rolled my eyes, losing my patience with this plan. "You seriously think that after what they did in Riverine, they won't be watching the border like crazy? They will have checkpoints every quarter mile, creatures patrolling with super-smelling capabilities. It's reckless, it won't work, and it will make us look like fools." I'd been taking battle strategy training since I was a child, from my own father. It was a bad plan.

My advisors didn't like my calling their plan reckless. I could tell by the steely gazes they were giving me.

"What do you suggest then, Empress?" Admiral Blade asked. "We shoot some fire over the Wall like usual and hope we hit something?"

He was condescending, and I didn't appreciate it.

'They will be watching the ground, but they won't be watching the skies,' Liana interjected.

I cocked my head to the side. *'What do you mean?'*

I had long come to terms with the fact that my creature could listen in on my conversations, or read minds, or both.

'I can fly, so can Onyx. We can deliver the payload to the Red Palace and blow it sky high.'

Chills raced the length of my arms. Kohen and I? Fly into Luska and blow up the Red Palace? It was crazy. Or genius. Or both.

"They won't be watching the skies. I could fly on my creature and deliver the explosive over the Red Palace," I told the surrounding men and women.

Eyes widened, mouths opened, and several 'No's' were uttered, but the commander appraised me with a head cocked. "You're our empress. You could not go alone."

I hated what I was about to suggest and how they would react to it.

"Kohen Badshah also has a flying creature," I said. The worst part was that I knew he'd do it, too. For me. For my dead father. For Amersea.

The room exploded into disagreement.

"You want us to trust a Badshah with protecting our empress?" Admiral Miraz admonished.

But again, the commander didn't completely balk at the idea. "How many men can your creature comfortably carry? *With* the payload."

'You, plus one other, plus the heavy explosive,' said Liana.

"Just one other plus the explosive," I relayed.

"And Badshah?" the commander asked.

'Three men, including Kohen,' Liana said, and I told the war room.

"Does Kohen have to go? Do you? Can we just borrow your creatures instead?" Elaine asked, clearly worried for me.

"It's a good question," Admiral Caruso agreed.

'I will do as you ask of me, Aisling,' Liana said, and I felt her loyalty through the bond. She wouldn't like it, but she would act like a horse and carry whatever I asked of her.

But I could never do that. There was no way in hell I was sending my creature into Luska alone with some strangers.

"No," I growled. "If we do this plan and send our creatures into danger, then Kohen and I will lead the mission."

One by one the advisors bristled.

"We've just lost our beloved emperor. Now we are supposed to be okay with sending our new empress into enemy territory with a few trained men?" Elaine asked, keeping her voice sharp and strong. But I saw the agony in her eyes.

Commander Ledger sighed. "Lieutenant Steele is right. It's a huge risk. I hate to have this conversation so quickly, but have you chosen a successor? One of your sisters will need to be taken under your wing and begin her training."

Before I could even open my mouth, Elaine puffed her chest up. "*All* three of the triplets have been raised to rule this country since they could walk. Empress Aisling will name her successor when she's ready, and of course, their training will be accelerated now that the emperor is gone."

She'd taken offense to the question, which I understood. It was her job to raise us up for this position, a job she took very seriously. I was glad she'd jumped in because I wasn't yet ready to say which of my sisters should be the next leader should I perish. By right of birth, it was Valor's place to rule, but I could overturn that if I thought someone else was ready. They were all babies; it was a hard thing to even think about. I'd wanted them to have what I didn't.

A childhood.

"I will fly home tonight, speak to Kohen Badshah, and then we can be back here in twenty-four hours to run the mission tomorrow night. You can work on the details in my absence."

The advisors exchanged nervous glances. Flying a large explosive deep into enemy territory was terrifying, but it would be worth it. They idolized their beloved Red Palace, and leveling it would be the perfect retribution for taking my father's life—for shattering the peace that Riverine once had.

"That was an order," I said. My first order, one of many I would issue. It was a good plan, and they were only hesitant because they cared about losing me, which was a good sign that they would grow to be as loyal to me as they were to my father.

"See you in twenty-four hours," the commander said, and just like that, the mission was approved, and I'd survived my first war meeting.

Now I had to go break up whatever I had started with Kohen and then ask him to risk his life for his country.

I felt like I was going to throw up.

CHAPTER TWO

It was just after eight p.m. As I flew home, fatigue pulled at my limbs. My night wouldn't be over for hours. I still hadn't even spoken to my sisters or Tetra. Everything had happened so fast.

'Is Kohen still following us?' I asked Liana. I had a handheld radio hooked to my belt; Elaine had the receiver in the car below. I had convinced her to let me fly on ahead because I could get home quicker with Liana not having to follow the roads. The distance between the radios had only a few miles before they lost connection, so I wasn't even sure I could call Elaine if I needed her. I think it just made her feel better, and so I'd hung on to it.

'Yes, he and Onyx are at a distance.'

The fact that Kohen thought he was my own personal bodyguard would be kind of charming under other circumstances. This was going to hurt. Remembering the sexy kiss we shared in the hallway at the graduation ball had an ache forming in my chest. Kohen was a weakness I couldn't afford.

Liana and I passed a dense stretch of woods. *'Tell him to land over there and meet us,'* I told her and pointed out an open patch of grass away from any roads or villages or signs of life. I wanted to tell Kohen that whatever we had started was done and get it over with. We were just professional colleagues now.

Liana landed, and I slipped off of her and paced the meadow. Reaching up, I touched my lips and tried not to think about how Kohen had kissed them only a day before. How could so much change in twenty-four hours?

I'd planned to have a mildly passionate love affair with Kohen until my father found out and threatened to kill us both before forcing me to marry someone of better breeding. Now that was definitely not going to happen. I was officially living under a microscope, and though Kohen was a sworn member of the Imperial Fleet, he'd never be good enough to be seen as a partner for me. In fact, if anyone saw us together romantically now that I was the empress, it would be a public relations nightmare. He was a Badshah, after all. His father's son. The man who took thousands of Amersean lives. A terrorist.

My stomach ached when I thought about what I was giving up without even being able to have it first.

I didn't even hear him land until the sound of his footsteps was behind me.

I pulled up every single wall I could around my heart and spun. Even so, the sight of his handsome face peering down at me with concern, his chiseled muscles pulling at the fabric of his black shirt, caused my stomach to bottom out and my heart to constrict.

"Thank you for meeting me," I said formally and held my hands clasped in front of me, fingers laced together.

He slowed, his gaze cautiously running over my body like a physical caress.

"Of course, Aisling. Are you okay?" My name on his lips was like a reverent prayer.

I cleared my throat. "I'm fine. But I needed to talk to you about a few things privately."

He stepped closer to me, and I stepped back from him, causing his brows to bunch together in the middle of his forehead. "Why are you acting weird?" The hurt in his voice killed me.

I straightened my spine. "Kohen, whatever romantically may have started with you and I has to stop now. I'm empress, and unfortunately a relationship between us would not be accepted by my people."

"*Our* people," he corrected, and it felt like he'd reached into my chest and squeezed my heart. "Aren't the Imbrians your people, too, now?"

Shame colored my cheeks. "Of course they are. But..."

Why was he making this hard? "Your father, and in turn, *you*, are not an acceptable match for me." I kept it short and to the point.

He grinned, and it caused my stomach to flop over. Why was he smiling, and why did he look so handsome doing it? He took another step forward, and I stepped back again until my butt hit the trunk of a tree.

"Then we will make them accept us," he declared.

He grasped the fingers of my uncasted hand, unlacing them as he stroked my palm with his thumb, sending waves of warmth throughout my body. My eyelids fluttered as my heart hammered like a war drum.

"They won't," I told him. "And neither will the Fleet or my advisors, or Elaine, or—"

He leaned in, his hot breath on my neck. "Then we'll hide it from them," he whispered, dragging his lips across my skin, which left a trail of fire in their wake. I whimpered, gripped by a throbbing need.

"Kohen," I panted.

"Yes, my Empress."

Oh stars, that nearly undid me right there. In all the grief of the last twenty-four hours, Kohen Badshah was my one bright spot.

"This won't end well," I told him as he peppered kisses along my collarbone, and I wrestled my hands free to thread them into his hair. Kohen pulled back, meeting my eyes with his blazing blue ones.

"Yes it will. It ends with you as my wife, Aisling."

I gasped, and then his lips were on mine, scorching, hard, insistent. That was a lie. It had to be. Bedding Kohen, I could believe. But *marrying* him? It would never happen. Not in a million years. Now I knew he wasn't truly seeing the future clearly. Maybe some things he did, like when he knew I would break my wrist or the attack on the training center, but I wondered if his visions were clouded by desires. His tongue stroked mine, and I moaned as I deepened the kiss, pressing my pelvis into him. I was just about to reach up into his shirt when something he said at the imperial graduation ball came back to me. I pulled away, panting. "Wait... last night..." I could hardly believe it was just last night. "...you said that was the last time you would kiss me for a long time. We're kissing now. A day later."

He chewed at his lip and nodded. "I think that sometimes I see things out of order. I'm still learning how to piece them together on the timeline. I thought it was—"

I frowned. "So your visions can change?"

He shook his head. "No, I don't think so. But I might get the timing wrong if I think I'm seeing something that happens more recently, and it's really farther in the future."

It sounded like he could be wrong about the future, but I didn't want to press him.

That reminded me of the other thing I had been wanting to ask him. "Kohen, would you ever lie to me?" I asked him.

He bristled, going stiff. "What?" He sounded hurt.

I swallowed hard. "Would you ever lie to me?" I wanted him to answer.

He seemed to consider my question and nodded. "If it meant keeping you from harm, I would." He stood taller at that, and I was taken aback by his raw admission. "What's this about?"

I felt my shoulders drop. I didn't want to know the answer to the next question. "You saw that someone I loved died. You said you didn't know who it was, only that I was sobbing over them. Is that true that you didn't know who it would be?"

His face flushed, and he swallowed hard. I knew from just looking at him that it was a lie. Whatever grief he'd chased away with that kiss was back in full force. "You *knew* my father was going to die!" I shouted into his face. "And you didn't tell me! I could have kept him hidden away, or I could have stopped the killer!"

He reached for me, but I backed away from him, slipping to the side, trying to calm the storm of emotions that had risen within me.

"Aisling, listen to me." His voice was steady. "I've said this before, but *everything* I do is to protect you." His eyes swam with emotion. "And not telling you that your father was going to die *was* protecting you."

What the hell did that mean? Would I have been emotionally impacted more by my father's death if I had known beforehand? Maybe if he told me and I wasn't able to stop it, I would be. It might have broken me to know I couldn't protect my father.

"I don't need your protection!" I screamed at him as fat, hot tears rolled down my face. He pulled me into his arms, and I let him crush me against his chest. "Yes you do. Trust me, you do," he breathed against my hair.

I let it all out then. In the safety of his arms, I broke down. It had been drilled into me my entire life that I had to be strong, to not show emotion. Emotions were weak. Love was weak. *I* was weak.

But maybe it was okay to be weak just this once, to allow myself to grieve the loss of the only parent I had... *just this once*. The sob shook my chest as I wept into his neck, and he stroked circles on my back, holding me with a strength that made me feel safer than I ever had in my entire life.

It felt like our fates fused together in this moment. Being this emotionally raw and vulnerable with someone... it bound you in a way, whether you wanted it to or not. Already, I was dreaming up ways to keep him, even if just in secret.

When I was all cried out, and it felt like the river had run dry, I pulled away and wiped at my eyes. Taking in a deep, calming breath, I shored the walls around my emotions up again and stiffened my posture.

I was the empress of all of Amersea. I couldn't break down like that ever again.

"There's something I have to ask you," I told him, changing the subject.

He nodded. "I will fly with you to blow up the Luskin Red Palace."

I gasped. "Liana told Onyx?"

He grinned and tapped his head. "I saw it."

A thrill went through me. "You saw us do it in a vision? Were we successful?"

"I thought you didn't want to know the future?" he asked with a raised eyebrow.

"Kohen," I warned. "I'm your empress now. Tell me if we are successful."

He gave me a playful smile. "Yes, Empress. We blow that building sky high. Now, whether we make it home safely or not, I haven't seen," he said, but there was something in his face that told me there was more to the story.

"And what else aren't you telling me?" I asked.

He shook his head. "Nothing."

"Kohen, I know you by now. You have a look. Why?"

Kohen just watched me with curiosity. "It's just that... today, you didn't fly over Imbria," he said, and I frowned.

"What? Why would I?"

He looked like I'd just shot him in the chest with an arrow. "I thought that now that Imbria was a part of Amersea and you were empress, you might fly over it to show the people you stood for them, too."

His words caused cracks to form in the walls I'd just erected. They tore a hole into my heart.

Why hadn't I flown over Imbria? Even the border? Were the people there even aware of what had happened to my father? Did they care? Did they even want me to fly over? I was basically their empress by force. Or at least that's what I'd been told.

"I… didn't think anyone would be outside to see me," I told him honestly.

He shrugged. "Only one way to find out."

I frowned. "Kohen, it's almost bedtime. I highly doubt the people of Imbria are staying up, waiting to see me in the skies."

Hurt crossed his face, followed by anger. "You'll never accept them as yours, will you?"

I shifted on my feet. "Of course they're mine. I will protect them if attacked, but—"

"But that's it. That's an ally, Aisling, *not* a leader." He shook his head in disappointment. "We should get back. It's getting late," he spat.

An ally, not a leader. That stung because it was true. Before I could say anything more, he got onto Onyx and then took off for the skies, leaving me to stew in my regret.

'Why the hell would I fly over Imbria? They hate us,' I asked Liana as I crawled onto her back, my mind spinning with everything Kohen and I had just discussed.

'Maybe so that they wouldn't hate you anymore. You are their empress, after all, and this is the empress parade, is it not?'

Dammit, she and Kohen were right.

I was keenly aware that one moment might change everything. I'd been spoon-fed a certain narrative about Imbria my entire life. It was time to find out if that was true.

'Head for the Imbrian border,' I told her, and she veered her course that way.

'What about Elaine and the admiral following you by car? They will expect you back in Riverine at an appointed time.'

I shrugged. *'I'm the empress. I don't ask permission to do things I want to do.'*

I could feel Liana's approval. But I should at least tell them so that they didn't worry. Pulling the handheld radio from my waistband, I depressed the button on the side.

"This is Firebird." I used the code name Elaine had given me. Not very subtle.

"Go ahead, Firebird." Elaine's voice was laced with worry.

"I have a private detour to make. There is a guard with me and I'm safe. Don't stay up." I then turned the radio off so that I couldn't hear the earful Elaine was no doubt giving me, empress or not.

'Is Kohen still trailing us?' I asked her.

'Yes. He's shocked you are actually going to Imbria. He's staying out of sight for your reputation's sake.'

I wish I didn't have a reputation. I wish I didn't have the

responsibility and title that meant Kohen couldn't get too close to me in public. I wished I could give it all up for him.

The last thought shocked me. It let me know I'd fallen deeper for him than I thought.

That was dangerous. I'd fallen in love with Jace, and look where that had gotten me. Cheated on.

But Kohen wasn't like that. With Jace, things were surface-level, puppy love. With Kohen, everything felt deeper, stronger. It scared me.

It was almost midnight when we flew over the Wilds. I could feel the heat of the fire sky above us and the ember rain around us. I'd never flown over the Wilds like this. It was beautiful.

Liana glanced up at the fire sky longingly, and I felt something rush through her and into our bond. Grief, pure and raw.

I stroked the feathers around her neck, waiting for her to tell me what that was about, but she never did, and I didn't press her. Liana had a complicated and long history. She was so old, with so many memories. I didn't ever pry for her to reveal them.

We crossed the river that split the two sides of the Wilds, the Amersea side and the Imbrian side, and I sat up straighter. I'd never been this far. I could see lights on the horizon just outside the densely packed forest of the Wilds on the Imbrian side, and as we neared, nervousness balled in my stomach.

I'd never been to Imbria. My father had never seen it as important enough to bring me. They were a conquered people. We used them for labor and resources, and otherwise, they kept to themselves.

As we neared the small border town, Liana flew lower. I searched the ground for some sign of people, but I knew it was probably futile. It was so late, and we were still in a fragile truce. I gasped when I saw the Amersea flag at half-mast. They'd lowered the flag for my father? It was probably some of the Imperial Fleet that lived in the small mining town that convinced them to do it. But the closer we flew, the more I noticed little specks on the rooftop of the apartment building. The specks had glowing lights...

When the scene came into view, my throat tightened. The rooftop was packed with people of all ages, *all* Imbrian. They held glowing candles and clanged pots and pans as they saw me near. There were about fifty people in all, a small town with a tiny population, but it looked like nearly everyone was in attendance on this rooftop.

As I flew lower, I could hear them screaming.

"It's the empress!" a little Imbrian girl in a bright pink silk wrap dress shouted as her father hoisted her up onto his shoulders.

The people cheered wildly as Liana flew circles above them, and I waved stupidly, in shock that it was past midnight and they'd waited up for me. Tears threatened to run down my cheeks, but I sucked them back. I'd been emotional enough for one day. It gutted me that they'd been waiting this entire time, and I hadn't intended to show. Would they have slept up here? Waited all night?

'Give them a show,' I told Liana.

She tipped her head to the side, and a stream of fire flew from her lips. The pots and pans clanged even louder as the children screamed joyously into the night.

They didn't seem like they hated me...

Were more towns in Imbria like this? Or was it only because they were on the border and we had the most interaction with them?

Liana's voice of reason cut through my thoughts: *'I cannot advise that we go deeper into Imbrian territory without a large Imperial Fleet escort.'*

I nodded, dashing any plans of an all-night flyover.

'But we can stop here if you'd like to meet these people?' she suggested. *'Word will spread that you came, that you cared.'*

I did care. I didn't know how much until this moment. The Imbrian people were my people. I'd been stupid to think of them as separate. For the first time since my father died, I questioned some of the things he'd told me about them.

'Okay, lower us down.' Elaine would kill me if she knew I was in Imbria about to speak to fifty civilians without a security detail.

Well, I had Liana. *And* I could control minds. And Kohen was somewhere in the darkness watching. I knew it. I could sense him. So I wasn't totally defenseless.

'I can protect you among this many people,' Liana informed me.

When the Imbrians saw me step out onto the ground, the people of the small village came downstairs to greet me. They wore huge smiles and fancy clothes of colorful silk. Their faces were adorned with some ceremonial face paint, and the women's long hair was braided with white fragrant flowers tied to the end. It appeared that they had dressed up as if this were a treasured holiday. I was so touched I had a hard time keeping the emotion out of my voice.

"Thank you for staying up," I told them. "I am Empress Aisling." I clasped my hands together in a prayer pose, the way I knew they did in a traditional greeting. They mimicked the motion but also bowed deeply to me.

A female elderly woman stepped forward, and I noticed the little girl in the pink dress clinging to her side. "We didn't think you would come, but we heard there would be a flyover, so we thought we'd stay up and see," she told me.

"I knew you'd come!" the little girl interrupted, and I smiled down at her.

Crouching down to her level, I met the little girl's gaze. "Can you tell me something?" I asked her.

She nodded, looking very serious.

"Is it true that Imbria makes the best spiced tea in *all* the world?"

The little girl's eyes lit up, and she nodded. "My nani

does!" She yanked the old lady's hand, and the woman smiled down at the youngster.

"Empress Aisling, would you like to come in for some tea?" the woman asked me, and the others nodded expectantly.

I swallowed hard. Such a simple offer, and yet it came with so many repercussions. The tea could be poisoned, and if I drank it and died, that would leave Amersea with a fourteen-year-old untrained empress in the form of one of my very immature sisters. But if I said no, it showed these people that I didn't trust them, and I didn't want that to be their first impression of me. Like Liana said, rumor would spread that I came to see them. I wanted to have tea with them, I *really* did, but I couldn't leave my family or my country without a leader.

"I—"

"She'd love to." Kohen's deep voice came from behind me, and I bristled.

The villagers looked up at him, and their eyes went wide. They clasped their hands and bowed to him, the same as they had to me.

"Prince Badshah," the elder woman said.

Interesting. They still called him "prince" and honored him in the same high regard they did me. It didn't bother me at all, but my father would have killed Kohen for it.

Kohen faced me and bowed deeply. "Empress, I've sent word via raven to Elaine and Admiral Caruso that there will be a slight delay in your plans to return home but that you are safe."

That was... thoughtful. And he was saying it out loud for all to hear, so that meant he was warning anyone here who had ill will against me that my people would know where to look for me. I'd already told Elaine I would be late, but I hadn't expected to land and have tea. She was probably furious. I'd pay the price for that later.

He looked at the old woman and rattled off something in his mother tongue and the woman glanced at me and smiled.

"What did you say?" I asked him, my mind spinning about the rumors that would spring from this. Kohen Badshah and Empress Aisling together in Imbria?

"I told her that I am your food taster and that I am hungry, so she'd better not poison me." Then he leaned in closer to me. "I also asked them not to tell others that I was here tonight."

I swallowed hard and gave a nervous laugh. "Of course they wouldn't poison you."

The woman gave me a knowing smile. "It would be my honor if you would come inside my home, Empress."

She led the way to a lower-floor apartment while the other residents pulled up chairs and tables outside. The second we entered the home, I was hit with the smells of amazing food. There were fragrant spices and roasted onion and stewed tomatoes. Even though I'd eaten earlier, my stomach growled and my mouth salivated. It was near midnight and yet a party had somehow begun. Live music blared to life outside, trays and trays of food began to appear, and I glanced around the home. It was small but clean, with light brown tile floors and clean white walls that held artwork native to the Imbrian culture. I was led into a tiny four-person dining room and requested to sit down by the little girl.

I did, and Kohen sat next to me as the older woman clanged around the kitchen.

A few others milled around the living room, talking, but kept their distance. The little girl leaned into me and whispered. "Is it true you got powers?"

I grinned and nodded once.

Her eyes widened. "Can I go into the Wilds one day and bond with a creature and get powers, too?"

"If you want to, of course," I told her. Though, I knew that she'd be less likely to get into the Lottery because she was Imbrian. I'd never really questioned that law until this moment.

I had a wild thought then. Maybe I could change the law. Have an even number of spots for Imbrians and Amerseans. We were one people after all, weren't we? Why not an even number in our Imperial Army? But even as I had the thought, I knew the admirals wouldn't go for it.

The older woman brought the tea to the table and poured the steaming liquid into four stainless steel cups. I noticed the amount she gave the little girl was only two mouthfuls. Enough to make her feel included, but not enough that she wouldn't sleep.

Kohen reached over to mine and took a swig. I saw his eyes fill with tears, and I straightened.

"Is it...?" *Did she poison him?*

"It tastes just like my mother's." He cleared the emotion from his throat and set the cup down before me.

I relaxed, shifting uncomfortably. We shared that, losing our mothers, and now neither of us had our fathers either. Orphans. We were orphans. The word felt so severe I didn't want to think it ever again.

After waiting for my tea to cool and to make sure Kohen didn't fall dead on his face from poison, I brought it to my lips and inhaled.

"Oh wow. It smells amazing." It was a rich, creamy brown color, with only a splash of milk, and smelled of clove and cardamom and something peppery. It smelled of Kohen.

Bringing my lips to the cup, I took a sip. The bright, aromatic flavor of tea and spices splashed across my tongue, and the warmth ran down my throat. It was incredible, spicy but sweet at the same time.

"I love it," I told the woman, and she smiled at my compliment.

"Are you hungry?" she asked us both.

We nodded, and then she proceeded to feed us a four-course meal at midnight because why not?

I waited for someone to bring a fork or spoon, but Kohen took a bite from each item on my plate by using his hands, so I figured I would do the same. When he gave me the all-clear, I popped in a cube of chicken coated in red cream sauce, and my eyes bulged as I coughed.

"Aisling!" Kohen said, alarmed.

I waved him off, and the grandmother appeared concerned as well.

"Spicy," I croaked.

"This isn't spicy! She's like a baby," the little girl said, and the entire table erupted into laughter, including me.

"Oh, I'm sorry, Empress, here." She spooned more creamed rice onto my plate to make everything milder.

A few moments later, Kohen laughed at me when I used a torn piece of flatbread to sop up some lentils, and it wound up in my lap.

"Shut up, I'm still learning," I scolded him under my breath.

"Nani, she said *shut up*," the little girl tattled on me, and I winced.

The grandmother, who I had learned was named Chara, tried to hide her smile. "She did. I'll have to make her do dishes for that."

The little girl burst into laughter, followed by the whole table.

"I will if you want me to," I told her seriously. I wasn't above doing dishes, especially if that was the house rule for cursing. Though I didn't technically think of *shut up* as a bad word.

The grandmother shook her head, trying to hide a smile. "I wouldn't dream of it, Empress."

Kohen watched me with an expression I could only interpret as adoration. I squirmed under that gaze because I felt it on my skin like a physical touch.

"Here." Kohen reached out and put his fingers over mine, showing me how to scoop up the food with the flatbread. "Like this."

My heart hammered in my chest as he brought it to my mouth, and I took the large bite.

"There are less dishes with no utensils," I said through my mouthful, and everyone was laughing again, including myself. How could I laugh when my father was dead? When I'd been grieving just this morning? It was these people, I decided. This humble home and the hospitality gave me a normalcy I'd craved my whole life. We tucked into our meal, and I allowed myself for just an hour to forget all of the seriousness waiting for me back home.

The food was amazing, but beyond the food, the company was the best. People took turns coming inside to greet me and introduce themselves. Some even brought small handmade crafts in the shape of my firebird creature. It filled up a part of myself I hadn't known was empty. I was so grateful we'd stopped here.

The next man who approached us I recognized as the one

who had put the little girl on his shoulders on the roof. He bowed to me with prayer-clasped hands and then faced Kohen. "Prince Badshah, if I could have a private word with you?" He was a sturdy man in his forties, with scars and sun damage to his skin. If I had to guess, I'd say he was an embersmith.

Kohen met my gaze, and I nodded.

"I'm sorry, but I cannot leave the empress' side. Whatever you have to say to me, you can say in front of her," he stated.

I peered at Kohen in surprise.

The man swallowed hard and nodded. "People in Nimra are saying things I thought you should know." He wrung his hands together nervously.

Nimra was the capital of Imbria.

"What are they saying?" Kohen asked.

The man eyed me apprehensively, and I braced myself. I had a feeling I wasn't going to like this.

"They are saying that now that the emperor is... no longer living... they want to gain independence again with you as our leader, as our king, like your father once was."

I stood so fast my chair skidded across the floor. The man bowed his head deeply.

"No offense was meant, Empress," the man muttered at my reaction.

"Gain independence *how*?" I asked him. "War?"

Could we handle a war with Imbria and Luska at once?

We'd done it before, but it would put a huge strain on our resources, and it had been decades.

What he'd said was treason. And Kohen leading *like* his father? That would make him a terrorist, too. I watched Kohen's face for any sign that he approved of this plan, but he appeared as shocked by the news as I was.

"My Empress..." The man bowed even deeper. "I'm merely a messenger, just sharing what the rumor is. I do not agree with their plan, but I thought you should know." He held out his hands in submission.

"I think it's time I leave," I told Kohen and everyone present.

The little girl was slumped over on the table, head cradled in her arms, fast asleep. The grandmother appeared dismayed that the night had ended this way. I was sorry it had as well.

"Thank you for the wonderful meal," I told her and clasped my hands together.

"It was my honor," she responded.

I turned my back on them then and made my way out to Liana.

What had started as a lovely night with a people I'd been wanting to know more about my entire life had turned into a sick feeling in my stomach. If Imbria rose up against me, I wasn't sure I was ready to fight two wars on two different fronts. I didn't want to hurt them; I wanted to welcome them to Amersea in a way my father never did. But maybe this was the proof my naivety needed.

I walked to the road, where Liana and Onyx waited. Kohen followed after me. Reaching for my arm, he turned me to face him. My chest was heaving. I was so upset. Everyone else had dispersed, making their way back to their homes, but I was stuck staring into Kohen's impossibly blue eyes with a horrifying question on my lips.

"Have you seen it? Have you seen Imbria attack Amersea?" I asked him.

He looked saddened by my question and shook his head. "No, Imbria doesn't attack Amersea first."

I frowned. "What do you mean *first?*"

Kohen let out a deep breath and held my gaze. "Aisling, I wish I could just fast forward us to when everything is better and we are together."

I shook my head. "That's not how life works."

He nodded. "I know." Then he looked out at the lights off in the distance, another town. "My little brothers are so close. I wish I could see them," he said wistfully.

His brothers? That shocked me. I'd forgotten he had two little brothers.

"Where do they live?" I asked, suddenly distracted by what he'd said as my earlier anger fled. Though I intended to circle back around to what he had said.

"They used to be in a rundown government school in

Nimra, but when we started boot camp and I got my first Fleet paycheck, I sent them to a nice boarding school in Sorak. It's just over there." He pointed to the lights in the distance.

He was telling me where he had stashed his little brothers away? That was something you only did with a person you trusted. "Well, you should go see them," I said, and then I got back to the topic at hand. "Kohen, what do you mean that Imbria doesn't attack Amersea *first*?"

Kohen glanced at Onyx as if he was itching to ride him away from here so that he wouldn't have to answer me.

"*You* attack Imbria first, Aisling. You lead an angry mob of soldiers into our land, and you burn a lot of it down."

I gasped. "I would never! Why?"

Kohen reached for my hands and then thought better of it. There were still people milling around. "There are so many things I want to tell you, but you won't believe me. If I tell you, it will make things between us worse."

I frowned. "What? Try me."

He shook his head vigorously. "No. I've made that mistake before. You'll just have to figure things out on your own. It's better that way."

I growled because what he'd said was so annoying. "Do you want to be king? To lead your people like your father did?" I asked him, thinking back to what the man had said.

He didn't answer right away, and I knew that it meant he did. Was he just using me? Making me soft towards him so that I would give him his kingdom back? Because I'd do that over my dead body.

"I wouldn't shy away from leadership if the opportunity fell into my lap, but my loyalty is to you first, Aisling. Then to Amersea, the Fleet, and Imbria last."

I gasped at the declaration. Me first? That was a bold thing to say. It was the *right* thing to say. Maybe he knew that.

"Because I'm your empress?"

He shook his head and stepped closer to me, letting his breath brush against my ear. "Because I'm in love with you," he whispered.

I stood there in complete shock as he then walked over to Onyx, slid one leg over her back, and took for the skies.

Did he... did Kohen Badshah just say he loved me?

CHAPTER THREE

I tore after him, leaping onto Liana and flying in Onyx's wake before pulling up alongside them.

"How dare you say that to me!" I screamed at Kohen.

He looked over at me with surprise. "Say what?" he yelled over the wind.

"I love you!" I screamed.

He shot me a half-cocked grin. "You do?"

I rolled my eyes. "No. You can't say you love me!"

He shrugged, seemingly unperturbed by my outburst.

"I love you!" he shouted back unflinchingly.

I growled. *This man!* He was so annoying and so adorable at the same time.

"Where are you going?" I realized we were flying away

from Riverine and deeper into Imbria, where those lights were. To Sorak.

"To see my brothers like you suggested. Come with me!" he yelled as Onyx and Liana tried to fly close enough so that we could speak but not so close that their wings touched.

It was so late. The middle of the night. And he wanted me to go deeper into Imbria? To meet his brothers? *It could be a trap.*

"It's a small upscale town with a lot of aristocrats who will likely all be sleeping. I'll protect you."

Why would I want to meet Kohen's little brothers? I was supposed to be breaking up with him...

I peered down at Liana, and I felt her assessing all the information through our bond. *'If it's a small town, I think we should be okay. If there is a mob of people, I'll simply fly you home.'*

Oh, Elaine was going to kill me.

"Why should I go with you?" I screamed back at him.

He met my gaze, the moonlight casting shadows across his face. "Because I want you to meet my brothers."

Why was I even entertaining this?! I'd had every intention of breaking up with Kohen today, and now we were flying to meet his brothers in Imbria? My father would roll over in his grave if he saw me... but there was an allure to Kohen that dragged me to him like a moth to a flame. Did his brothers look like him? Were they taught to hate me? Would my going there make them think we were a couple? *Were* we a couple?

I had a thousand questions and no answers.

"Okay!" I shouted and followed his lead. My curiosity to see more of Imbria and what his brothers looked like won over all rationality.

We flew over green rolling hills and then small villages that were in disrepair until we reached the cluster of lights that designated the city of Sorak. It was huge and entirely fortified. The lights were coming from outside a giant wall. There was a glowing sconce every six feet that ran in a circle around the entire fort. The second we flew lower, I noticed that this city didn't hold the signs of war the others did. Sorak was well protected, with a huge stone wall around it that came up like a dome; only the top was open to let in some light. We flew down into the open top, which seemed small at first, but as we went through, I realized the opening was hundreds of feet wide.

I gasped when we dropped down over the city. It was incredible. Small, neat rows of houses ran in concentric circles around the outer edge, with a beautiful park inside the center and some larger buildings dotting its edges. I peered up at the sky and was taken with how beautiful it was. The moon was directly over the center hole in the dome, and now that I was inside the city, I noticed a few stones were missing in the covering to let a glimpse of stars and moonlight through. It was an incredible marvel of architecture.

I peered back down and lost sight of Kohen for a second until Liana caught up with him. He was lowering Onyx at the edge of the park near a large, beautiful estate.

Sorak Boarding House for Boys, the sign read in front of the white stone building. There was no one outside. Considering it was late and everyone should be sleeping, I wasn't too surprised. I was, however, in shock at how beautiful this place was. And Kohen could tell. He was watching me keenly as Liana landed beside Onyx.

"What do you think?" he asked.

I shook my head in wonder. "It's amazing. I... didn't know Imbria had places like this." I was embarrassed to admit that. I was slowly realizing how much I'd judged the Imbrian people and their land with preconceived notions my father had taught me.

His jaw clenched. "All of Imbria was like this before the Occupation."

The Occupation. I didn't want to argue about that, so I just nodded. "No guards at the gates?" I noticed we weren't stopped.

Kohen scoffed at that. "Who would guard us? The Imperial Fleet? Your father ordered the Imbrian army disbanded when he took over. We have no protection but what you designate."

My chest constricted at that. Yes, technically Imbria was

now a part of Amersea, a state in a country if you will, but we didn't treat it as such. We didn't allocate an even percentage of our resources here like we did in Riverine. I felt so conflicted at that moment that I just wanted to leave. I was already so overwhelmed at becoming empress and my father's death... I didn't have the mental and emotional bandwidth to confront all of my father's decisions of the last decade.

Just as I was going to suggest I leave, Kohen reached for my hand, stroking my palm with his thumb. "I want you to meet Tej and Arjun. It's important."

It's like he knew I was thinking about leaving.

"Your brothers?" I asked. "Do you speak to them often?"

He nodded. "I send them any spare money I get from the Fleet, and in two years, my brother Tej will be old enough to enter the Lottery. Then Arjun will be two years behind him. Assuming they get their names picked."

Tej. Arjun. Hearing their names made them real.

"Do you want them to get picked?" I asked as he led me around the side of the building.

He looked at me like I'd grown two heads. "Of course I do, Aisling. The only way left to make any decent money in Imbria is to join the Fleet."

That made an ache form in my chest. I yanked his hand, forcing him to stop and look me in the eye. "If you want your brothers' names to be called, I'll make sure they're called," I promised. I'd rig the Lottery for him.

Oh man, I had it bad.

This dark-skinned, blue-eyed dream of a man had lured me to him like an animal in a trap. I still had yet to figure out if his trap would kill me or set me free.

He gave me a small smile and squeezed my hand before letting go. There was something about that smile that said he knew more on that. Like maybe he'd had a vision about it. Would I break my word and not get his brothers in the Lottery? I hated that he knew the future and I didn't.

He walked over to the third window and rapped his finger against it in a certain rhythm. Three times fast and two times slow. A moment later, the light turned on, and the curtain was pulled back. Then, I was confronted with a handsome mini-Kohen.

My gut clenched at the sight of the maybe fifteen-year-old boy. He tore the window open, grinning ear to ear.

"Get up, idiot. Kohen's here!" the young boy snapped at someone in the bed next to him. He leaped out the open window. Kohen tackle-hugged him and my heart pinched in my chest. Seeing the young boy with bronzed skin, wild dark hair, and piercing blue eyes shook me. But as I watched them, I noticed there was a stark difference between Kohen and Arjun. Arjun had a childlike joy, like maybe Kohen had shielded him from things when he was growing up. There wasn't a brokenness to him like I saw when I looked into Kohen's eyes.

When they pulled away, another boy about seventeen

years old appeared in the open window with his hair flattened to one side. He gazed sleepily at us all.

"Holy shit, that's the empress," he said and seemed to perk up a little, appearing more awake.

This must be Tej. He had more of a hardened look in his eye, like Kohen.

"It is?" Arjun asked, eyeing me for the first time. "Should we bow?" The young teen looked at his eldest brother.

"No, that's fine," I said, but at the same time Kohen said, "Yes."

Arjun made prayer-clasped hands and bowed deeply to me, obeying his elder brother. Tej did the same, but warily.

"Nice to meet you," I said nervously.

Why was I here?

Tej leaped out the window and eyed me from feet to head. "I didn't think you'd fly over Imbria, or we would have stayed up."

There was a veiled diss in there. Like I didn't think Imbria was good enough to fly over. I couldn't fault him, though—I hadn't intended to.

Before I could respond, Kohen cleared his throat. "Aisling isn't here as empress. She's my friend, and I wanted you to meet her."

"Why?" Tej asked.

Awkward. I was wondering the same thing.

"Because it's important to me," was all Kohen said, and I shifted awkwardly on my feet.

What was he doing? It was like I'd come to meet the family of a guy I was seriously dating, but we weren't seriously dating.

Right?

"Why?" Tej pressed.

"Because one day you will serve her, and I want you to respect her like I do. She's not her father."

My knees went weak. Not that there was anything wrong with my father, but he'd just paid me a huge compliment, and teaching his brothers to respect and follow me as their leader was about the hottest sign of loyalty I'd ever seen.

"Fine," Tej shrugged.

"Are you guys friends?" Arjun asked as we began to walk to the back gardens.

Please, for the love of every star in the sky, just say, 'Yes', I begged Kohen with my gaze. Telling his brothers that I would one day be his wife or any of the other insane things he'd told me would not be smart. He could believe those delusions, but I didn't want him spreading them around.

"Yes," Kohen said. "We are the only two in the Fleet that have creatures we can fly on, so we get sent on missions together."

Oh, that was good. I nearly sighed in relief.

"Are you important in the Fleet?" Arjun asked his brother and looked excited at that prospect.

Before Kohen could speak, I interrupted him.

"Very," I told them both. "We have a mission coming up

that only Kohen and I can do because of our special skills." I tried to be vague so as to not compromise the mission.

"That's cool," Arjun said, kicking a rock and watching it roll away.

"What are your powers?" Tej asked, sitting down on a bench and yanking a flower from the ground, pulling petals off of it as he looked up at me.

"I'm immune to flame—"

"Like my brother!" Arjun said. He was so excited I couldn't help but smile.

"Yes, and I can... blow up, kind of like a bomb," I added, and Tej stopped pulling petals off the flower and peered up at me open-mouthed. Arjun was speechless too, so I gave a nervous laugh, and then they both broke into a rapid-fire commentary and questions of, *"No way, so cool. Can you show us? Have you ever blown anyone up?"*

Kohen was laughing by the time they were done.

"Okay, okay, let her breathe," he said because Arjun had stepped closer with each question, eagerly awaiting my response. I had to admit, he was adorable. A young and innocent version of Kohen without the tattoos and broken soul bleeding through his eyes. Kohen had seen things in his life, and probably Tej too, but they'd shielded Arjun from it all. It made me sad.

I changed the subject. "How do you like living here?"

"It's way nicer than the government school, but the kids are stuck up," Arjun said.

Tej rolled his eyes. "Who cares if the kids are stuck up? We get three hot meals a day and clean sheets."

A pang of sadness ran through me at that. Did their last school not have three hot meals a day or clean sheets?

Tej glanced at me, reading my face. "Has the empress ever gone without a meal?" There was a bitterness in his tone. I knew I hadn't fully won him over yet. Not that I was trying.

"Way to ruin the mood," Arjun scolded his brother.

"Tej," Kohen warned. "Of course she hasn't. She's the empress and was raised without want for anything. As it should be," Kohen told them both.

"You're wrong," I said to Kohen. "I often went three days without any food as a part of my training for the Wilds." I could still remember being fifteen years old and lying awake as my stomach felt like it was eating itself. The craziest thing is after two days, the hunger just goes away. As if it knows it won't be getting anything, it gives up.

All three of their eyebrows shot up.

"Three days?" Arjun said.

"For training? That's messed up!" Tej commented.

I squirmed a little under their gaze. My father wanted to make sure I was ready for anything, and so even against Elaine's consultation, he made me go without food often. For training, of course.

"Being trained to be empress isn't all glory and riches," I

declared. Though I did have a nice life with all the comforts, so I wasn't complaining.

When I looked up into Kohen's eyes, I could see an inferno of emotions there. He looked mostly *angry*...

A yawn escaped me then, and I covered it. "I should be getting back. I still haven't checked on my sisters."

Kohen nodded, giving his brothers a hug. "Mind the teachers, and don't get in trouble. I'll send more money when I can."

Tej shook his head. "You already overextended yourself paying for this place. I have ways of making money."

Kohen pinned Tej with a glare. "You will *not* steal for money. I will send you money next paycheck. Stay out of trouble until then."

Steal? Was the Fleet not paying enough for Kohen to take care of his brothers and himself? I'd have to look into how much we paid entry-level soldiers. Though this place looked nice. I was glad he was able to get them here.

Tej rolled his eyes and grumbled, "Fine."

He and the triplets would get along well, I decided. They both had sass.

After bidding them farewell, we went out front, where our creatures were waiting. Something about coming and meeting his brothers felt a little off to me. Like Kohen was going out of his way to get them to like me. And for what? *Who cares?* I liked meeting them, but I wanted to know if he had a motive behind it.

"Why were you making me sound so good to them?" I asked him before we saddled up to ride home.

Kohen glanced over at me with those handsome blue eyes, and my stomach warmed.

"Well, first of all, you *are* good. Secondly, one day it will be important that my brothers like you."

A chill broke out onto my arms, and he said nothing more. "Let's head back," he agreed, and we took to the skies.

He'd had a vision, and this was all to play into that. I decided right then and there that I wished Kohen had the power to control people and I could see the future. When I used my power, I took away a person's basic freedom, which felt awful. When Kohen used his, he knew everything, which put him at an advantage over me. It felt like we were playing chess, and Kohan was three moves ahead of me at every turn.

CHAPTER FOUR

I didn't expect anyone to be awake when I got to Tetra's at 4 a.m. But I needed to see my sisters and make sure they were okay. I was beyond tired and had reached a point of heightened clarity where my brain felt like it was buzzing. The second I stepped off of Liana, a shadow moved on the porch. I held my hands up, ready to fight, and then Elaine walked out into the moonlight with Vespa at her side.

"You went to Imbria?" she scolded me.

Old Aisling would apologize, but I was empress now. "Yes." I tipped my chin up. "They are my people, too."

Elaine sighed, resigned. She looked exhausted. "I've been worried sick. Let's get some rest. In the morning, we find a new house and move your sisters into it."

I nodded, and then the door opened. Tetra, my best friend, stood there looking disheveled. Her eyes were a bit puffy, like she'd been crying, and her hair was a mess. Elaine stepped off the porch with Vespa trailing behind her before she slipped into an unfamiliar car. I knew she'd waited up to make sure I'd gotten home safe.

"I'll see you in about three hours," Elaine said.

Three hours? I was going to be a dead woman walking.

I spun back to Tetra, who leaned on her cane as she stood to the side and allowed me into the house. I stepped into her small living room and peered at my best friend in the low light. Her bonded wolf, Ariyel, was curled up asleep at her feet.

"Do I have to bow to you?" she asked.

I grinned. "Hell yeah. Or I'll imprison you."

That got a small smile to grace her lips. "Can I... hug you?"

My throat tightened and I nodded once, opening my arms as she hobbled over and crashed into them.

I wrapped my arms around her, squeezing tightly as she held me back.

"Just because I'm empress doesn't change anything between us," I told her. She was my best friend in the whole world, and I needed something normal in my life for once.

She nodded and then pulled back to look at me. "I'm so sorry about your dad. Do you know who did it? Can you tell me?"

"Luskins. I'm not sure who. Probably the breath-stealing witch who rode the red dragon. I'll find out more when his bloodwork comes back. No poison in his stomach, so it wasn't likely one of our own."

She sighed in relief at that.

"How are my sisters?" I asked her.

She peered down the hallway to her house and winced. "Victory cried herself to sleep. Valor isn't talking. Virtue is acting like an eight-year-old again. They're scared you're going to die next. They are sleeping with my mom. They didn't want to be alone."

My heart seized in my chest. Everyone thought that twins or triplets were the same person. They weren't. My sisters might look identical, but they had very different personalities, and that evaluation Tetra had just given me was very accurate for each of them. Vic was my sweet one, so it made sense she'd be the first to cry. Valor was the heir, the one who thought she'd have to stay strong, so she was shutting down and not talking. And sweet Virtue probably didn't know what to do, so she just retreated into being a kid again.

This was the one thing I was unprepared for. I knew how to take over as empress for my father—I'd attend war meetings and even fight on the front lines. I knew the political games and how to play them, and what the next few years would entail as I fought to show my people I was strong enough to lead. But nothing could have prepared me to be a mother to my three sisters—to raise three fragile and emotionally unstable teenagers into fierce young women.

"I can't do this," I said suddenly and fell back against the wall, the exhaustion pulling at my limbs.

Tetra reached out with her cane and swatted my thigh. "Yes you can, because you have to!"

That was the depressing truth. *I had to.* There was no other choice.

I sighed.

"Ash?" Victory's singsong voice filtered through the room, and I looked up to see her at the end of the hallway. She wore her purple fuzzy pajamas and matching socks. She was so young, such a child still. I wanted her innocence to linger for another few years, but I knew it was already shattered.

"Is it true?" Her voice shook. "Is Father really dead? I mean, everyone is saying he is, but I thought that maybe..."

Oh no.

She was still in shock, in disbelief. I didn't want to do this right now, but like Tetra said, I had to.

"He is. He was killed late last night." Or was it the day before? Time was weird now that it was the middle of the night, and I hadn't slept. I pushed off the wall and walked over to her.

My little sister's sob ripped through Tetra's small home and shook me into action. I crossed the room and pulled her into my arms as she shook with grief.

"He loved you," I told her. "He just didn't say it." It was a nice thing to say. And I knew it was true. My father was a complicated man who just didn't know how to express himself without feeling weak. *Yes*. That was the truth. He *did* love us.

"What will we do!" Vic wailed into my shoulder.

I pulled her back and met her gaze. She looked like a tiny, frightened doe in the headlights of an oncoming train. "We will be strong. For Father. For each other. And for our country."

And just like that, her tears stopped. She sniffled and rubbed her eyes. "I'm tired," she said.

"Me too," I told her.

"Me three." Tetra yawned behind us.

We all walked down the hallway to Tetra's room. Ariyel followed us and then curled into a ball on the floor. I crashed into Tetra's bed first, Vic snuggled up into my arms, and then Tetra was last. Victory threaded her fingers through Tetra's, and the sight warmed my heart. My sisters had grown up knowing Tetra almost their whole life, and if anything did happen to me, I knew she would be there for them. With that thought on my mind, I fell fast asleep.

I WOKE about three hours later with the sun filtering through Tetra's window and anxious thoughts racing through my mind. I needed more sleep, but I wouldn't get it. I was running a country now. My father rarely slept, and now, neither would I.

I slipped out of bed without disturbing Tetra or Victory and made my way to the kitchen, where Bethel was brewing coffee. Valor sat at the table staring at a cup of milk, seemingly in a catatonic state.

I gave Tetra's mother, Bethel, a nervous glance, and she looked at me with all of the compassion and empathy of a mother who knew their child was hurting.

"Are you too important for a hug?" she asked, opening her arms. It occurred to me that everyone in my life that I cared about would now be scared to hug me or say something that they thought might upset me or even just be around me. I was *empress* now.

"Never," I told her and fell into her arms.

She rubbed my back as she held me, one of my favorite things, something she'd done since I was little, and then she released me.

"I have faith that you will lead us into peace and end this war," she told me boldly.

Peace? It wasn't something I'd ever considered or my father ever spoke about.

End the war, yes, we wanted to conquer the Luskins and put an end to the bloodshed, but peace? I hadn't ever thought about a peaceful end until now.

She went back into the kitchen, and I sat down next to

Valor. My sister was rigid, face forward, and barely seemed aware of my presence.

"It's okay to be scared, or sad, or whatever you are feeling," I told her.

She didn't look at me, just squeezed her hands together in her lap. "I'm oldest. I know what's expected of me now, Aisling." Her voice was monotone.

My heir. My successor. The one to run this country if I died. And she was all of fourteen. She'd barely just gotten her period last year. I couldn't expect this of her. And yet, the same had been expected of me. I'd lived my whole life as my father's successor. But I wanted more for her. I wanted her to have a carefree childhood before this crushing responsibility fell upon her.

I lowered my voice and leaned into her. "I can name Virtue my successor if you don't want it." We both knew Victory was too sweet and soft to rule the Imperial Fleet. Virtue was a blend of both of them.

Valor snapped her head in my direction, fire in her eyes. "I want it," she growled.

I smirked. Stars, she was so much like me. How had I never seen it before?

"Okay, then," I told her. "You will be my successor."

She looked excited and terrified all at once and then profoundly sad. "Aisling?"

"Yes?"

She leaned into me. "I heard you last night talking to Vic.

Father didn't love us. He tolerated us because we fit into his plan, but he didn't love us." Her voice was laced with fury.

I nearly slapped her. "*Don't* speak like that," I warned her.

How could she even think that?! She was always the rebellious one, like me. And here she was, going the anger route. Angry at a dead man. What good would that do?

There was a knock at the door, and I was grateful for the distraction. I stood to get it, but Bethel beat me to it. While she answered the door, I grabbed a cup of coffee and a thick slice of honeyed ham. This modest house in the suburbs was like a second home to me. These peach walls, the home-cooked food... it would always give me a warm feeling I would crave.

Elaine's voice reached me from the doorway: "You'll have to take that to go, Empress. There are urgent matters that require your attention." I sighed, shoving the ham into my mouth and raising the mug to Bethel. "Can I borrow this?" I said between mouthfuls.

She gave me a sweet smile and nodded.

I peered at Valor. "Take care of your sisters. I'll try to see you later this afternoon." I needed to be at Sky Reach by nightfall to execute the new plan, but I would try to see them once more.

As I followed Elaine out the door, I noticed her face was pulled tight, lips pursed into a thin line.

"What is it?" I asked her.

She held a clipboard and a piece of paper with many things written on it. I ducked into the family car, giving a greeting to Verik, and then stared at the seat my father always sat in with Zuri beside him. It was slightly baggy where his butt had carved a dent. Elaine cleared her throat behind me, and I stepped inside, sitting in my father's seat, feeling like an imposter. Vespa jumped in next, taking the seat on the bench across from me as Elaine slid in next to him.

'I'm right above you if you need me,' Liana said.

'Thanks,' I told her.

"I'm going to give you a quick rundown of things, and I need you to give me fast answers or we will be doing this all day," Elaine told me as the car took off.

I frowned. Straight to the point on three hours of sleep. That sounded like good ol' Elaine. "Okay. Shoot."

"Now that your father's rule is over, it's customary to switch out any staff you no longer feel would serve your best interests, and assign new staff in their place."

Oh. Wow. Fire people?

Okay, I hadn't been expecting that.

"First on the chopping block is Lucinda Lark," she said, keeping her face calm and unbiased, which was an incredible feat since I knew for a fact we both couldn't stand her.

"Oh my stars, can we fire her? I genuinely hate her," I said, and Elaine's lips curled into a smile.

"Done. Who would you put in her place? Someone who

can be good at public speaking and note-taking, and all of the things an assistant to an important figure will be required to do."

I chewed my lip. "Would it offend you if I offered you the position? Not because I want you to be my assistant, but Lucinda and my father spent a lot of time together, and I want you by my side as much as possible."

"I will work in whatever position you ask of me," she said with a small smile.

"Then I would like for you to replace Lucinda, but instead of assistant, let's call you senior advisor because that's what I really need."

That brought a smile to her lips, and she jotted it down. "Done."

She rattled off a dozen other staff members, and I chose to retain them all. Lucinda was the only one who bugged me. Her shrill voice and fake smile were grating, but the way she would stroke my father's arm and bat her eyelashes at him made me want to vomit in my mouth.

This conversation about hiring and firing people caused something to suddenly dawn on me. I turned to Elaine.

"Hey, remember Charline Wells? The one who let Tetra use her pack?"

She nodded and peered up at me. Vespa cocked his head to the side as well. It seemed they were both curious why I was asking about Charline.

"I gave her my word that one day, when I was empress, I'd make her a member of my personal guard. I hadn't expected to be empress so soon, but she's smart and a fast learner."

Elaine nodded. "If you gave her your word, you should honor it. I'll make sure her training is fast-tracked, and she's offered a nice position with a salary and benefits."

I relaxed at that. It was important to me to be a woman of my word, and Charline deserved the job. After Fleet training, even without a creature, she would be valuable to me. I valued loyalty. Verik took a turn out of Tetra's neighborhood and into a bit of a nicer area.

"Speaking of salaries, do you know how much we pay brand-new cadets like Anika and Tetra?" I asked.

"I can find the pay schedule somewhere for you. It's decent, but nothing that will have them looking ahead to retirement anytime soon."

"And they get paid the day they get back from the Wilds?" I asked her, slightly embarrassed I didn't know this myself.

She nodded. "So that they can get properly outfitted for boot camp."

I chewed my lip. I knew that allowing new candidates to get a chunk of ember in the Wilds was something we did to take the financial strain off, but what about those who couldn't? Like Kohen.

"Could we offer a small sign-on bonus to new candidates

when they graduate boot camp and head to their new posting?"

Elaine raised an eyebrow. "Your first big financial decision as empress. It will be in all of the papers by morning. Are you sure you want to do that?"

My stomach tightened at her assessment. Why was she saying it like that? I squirmed.

"What do you think?" I asked her.

She shrugged. "I want to know what *you* think."

I sighed. "Why can't you just tell me what to do?"

That got a smile out of her. "Because then you wouldn't learn. Come on, you've trained for this. Do you think it's a good idea on your first day in office to give hard-earned tax money to soldiers?"

I scoffed. "Soldiers that fight for the safety and lives of this country! Yes!"

She grinned as if I'd fallen into her trap. "Good. I agree. I'll have the treasury department come up with some numbers, and you can choose."

I relaxed at that. Thinking of Kohen's brother Tej saying he could steal to get by caused a lump to form in my throat. I hadn't expected what I'd found in Imbria last night; it conflicted with everything I'd been taught my entire life. The people were... kind to me... and the city of Sorak was beautiful and upscale, nothing like what my father told me, nothing like the pictures we saw in school. Not that being upscale mattered, but it kind of did. Our history books had painted a picture in my head of the Imbrians being unable to prosper without us. And now that I knew that wasn't true, I wasn't sure what to think.

We'd only been driving for a few minutes when the car stopped and the window rolled down. I found myself staring at a sizeable home for this area. It was set back a good way from the road, which afforded it privacy. It had a white picket fence and was painted a pretty blue. A huge willow tree marked the front yard and hid the garage and half the porch. It was nothing like my father's, not even grand like Jace's. It was still nice, though, and very private, which was important.

"This is a four-bedroom house, with an office, close to school for the girls, but also to Tetra's. The triplets can see Bethel every week. She has promised to tutor them in math and writing."

I nodded. Bethel was a smart woman and patient, too. She'd make a good tutor for the triplets, and they were already comfortable with her. It would also provide extra money for her. Elaine was sweet to offer her the position.

"It would fit you and the girls comfortably enough, but it's understated for someone of your rank and what you are accustomed to. I fear if we move you into a giant mansion, it will be too obvious. This way, only a handful of people would know about it. The backyard is large and full of trees, so Liana can land without being seen, and I'll have a guard-house built by the end of the month for round-the-clock security."

I nodded, seeing myself and my sisters here. It was a lovely little house, a modest home for an empress, which is why no one would look here.

'I like the backyard. It has a pool, too,' Liana said.

"Buy it," I told her.

"Do you want to go inside? I got the key for a private viewing. I said it was for myself."

I shook my head. "I'm sure we don't have time. It looks private, which is the most important." I just wanted to keep my sisters safe.

She nodded, scratching another thing off of her list. The car started up again, and we headed towards the center of the city as the sun fully rose.

"Have you found a replacement to train the girls and take care of their daily needs?" I asked her.

Elaine nodded once. "Sergeant Gwenivere Black. Goes by Gwen. Tetra is interviewing her later this morning."

I raised one eyebrow, grinning. "You are allowing my savage bestie to interview the triplets' new governess?"

Elaine shot me a half-cocked smile. "Who better to ferret out any weakness? I've already met with and approve of Gwen. Caruso has questioned her and her loyalty is with you. If Tetra approves, she's got the job."

Brilliant. I relaxed a little, knowing my sisters' needs were being taken care of.

Verik pulled out of the residential area of Riverine and headed for the more industrial part of town.

"Speaking of Tetra..." Elaine said, and I went still. There was something in Elaine's voice I didn't like.

"What about her?"

"Do you still want her to be a drill instructor at the training campus that was just attacked? Or would you like to take her with you to Sky Reach, where you will now be posted five out of seven days a week, with weekends off to see your sisters?"

I felt like I couldn't breathe. It was an impossible choice. Take Tetra to Sky Reach? It was a death sentence. But the thought of keeping her here, without being able to keep an eye on her, killed me.

"Can we honorably discharge her from the Fleet?" I asked, and Elaine gave me that look. The look that said I was being crazy.

"She would kill you. And she's not weak, so *don't* treat her as such," she scolded me.

I groaned, knowing she was right, and grateful she wasn't sugarcoating the way she spoke to me now that I was empress. There was something comforting about a verbal lashing from Elaine. "But I want to keep her safe," I protested.

Elaine nodded. "Then train her like I trained you. She's got a creature and, from what I hear, a tremendous power. Mold her into an invaluable soldier, and maybe in ten years, she will be commanding your army instead of Jace's father."

Whoa.

It was *such* an Elaine thing to say. Leave it to her to see Tetra's potential.

"Okay," I said nervously. "But only if she wants to," I added.

Elaine chuckled at that. "She already begged me to place her wherever you were going."

Which was such a Tetra thing to say. It made me love my bestie all the more.

The car made its next stop, and I went to peer out the window to see where we were when Elaine gently grasped my face and averted my gaze.

Her eyes bore into mine. "I saved the worst news for last."

My heart hammered in my chest. What news could this be? How much more could I take in my first few days as empress?

"The lab your father's blood results were sent to was burned down late last night. Someone is trying to cover up the murder."

I gasped, and she released my face. I tore away from her to see that the brick building that held our top medical lab filled with scientists and expensive equipment was a hollowed-out shell.

"Why? Why would Luska do this?" I asked as I felt an uneasiness churn in my stomach.

"Luska wouldn't," Elaine said. "They wouldn't care if we knew it was them."

No. It felt like the ground had opened up and swallowed me whole. The car spun as I tried to grapple with what this meant. If Luska didn't kill my father... it meant someone in the Imperial Fleet did.

Something in the blood results would point to them. My heart stopped when I realized that my father was scheduled to be cremated today. "Can we get more blood?" I asked Elaine quickly.

She nodded. "I've already ordered that his body be protected under constant guard and not cremated until you give word. We will get to the bottom of this."

Anger roiled through me. One of our own? Someone within these walls thought they could take my father out and live with it?

"I'll burn whoever did this to the ground," I growled and was surprised to see smoke rising off of my skin for a split second before vanishing out the open window.

Elaine placed a hand over mine, a rare show of affection from my mentor and now senior advisor.

"We have to prepare for the fact that you could be next," she said. "I want every single person you come into close contact with interrogated by Admiral Caruso. Everyone. Including me and Tetra."

I recoiled at that. "No way. The day I can't trust my own best friend and you is the day I don't want to live."

Elaine shook her head. "I want you to know for sure. This kind of thing can mess with you mentally. I want you to know Tetra and I are people you can trust because that list is going to grow very small, Aisling."

Her certainty scared me.

"I do know that I can trust you," I told her. Admiral Caruso was a human lie detector. It was her power and would be very valuable if someone in the Fleet killed my father, but I couldn't fathom Tetra or Elaine doing such a thing. My gaze went to Vespa, who sat next to Elaine. He did have poison fangs—no, I couldn't do that, I couldn't suspect family!

"Will you know that in two weeks' time when someone else is assassinated? Or there are a string of murders around you? We don't know how far this will go. This could be a coup to take the empire down."

Chills rose on my arms. I thought of last night when I'd gone to Imbria, and that man had told Kohen that the people wanted to be free again and have him lead them.

Could Imbria have done this somehow? My mind raced with different possibilities.

It would take Caruso months to sweep through the entire Imperial Fleet. Maybe even the better part of a year.

"Okay," I conceded. Elaine was smart; she would make a

good advisor. I hadn't thought of using Caruso. Why hadn't I thought of that?

"And I'll interrogate Caruso myself," Elaine added.

My eyebrows rose at that. "Interrogating an admiral? Is that smart?"

"Can you afford to spend time with someone on a daily basis that we aren't sure about? If you mandate the interrogation, I'm well within my right to do it." Her face betrayed something then like maybe it made her a little sick to do such a thing because she was close to Caruso.

I nodded. "But we will have someone else do it. I know you two are close."

"Interrogating" an admiral to ferret out the truth, involved some mild torture, I was quite sure. But who made sure that the person who could smell a lie wasn't telling lies themselves? For all we knew, Caruso wanted my father dead, then me, and she'd rule Amersea herself. I had to detach from the emotional aspect of all of this and just carry out the plans, even if it was hard.

Elaine shook her head. "I don't trust anyone else not to lie to me about the results, Aisling. *You* are my priority now."

I swallowed hard, hating that it had come to this. Elaine was going to torture Caruso to make sure she was loyal to the empire? Then Caruso was going to question all my friends? What would they think of me?

"Fine," I croaked.

With that, the car took off, and we were heading to a

familiar spot. My father's house. My childhood home. The emperor's palace.

"This will be a front for Riverine. We'll keep the lawn maintained. You and your sisters can make sparse appearances. Let people think you still live here. I'll have you and your sisters' rooms packed up and transferred to the new house, as well as your father's office. I'll do it in the dead of night so no one sees. Is there anything else you want specifically from here for the time being?"

This was all happening too fast. I just wanted everything to slow down a little so I could think. I had to be at Sky Reach by tonight to make a retaliatory attack on Luska. I'd be living and training there during the week and then flying back here on the weekends. I just wanted a break.

"No," I said finally and sat back against the seat.

This house was never really a home to me anyway. It was my father's, and I'd walked on eggshells here around him my entire life. It was for the best that we moved into this new place. Better to look forward instead of back.

"There's one more stop we have to make," Elaine told me. "Change into this while we drive there."

She pulled a knee-length black dress from a garment bag, and my stomach sank. It was a funeral dress, and suddenly, I knew where we were going.

CHAPTER FIVE

The car pulled up to the Riverine Imperial Fleet Cemetery just as the service began.

I counted twenty-six mounds of freshly churned earth to mark the deaths of those who fell at the attack on our training campus. I knew Nikhil was among one of them, and was reminded of his sacrifice to save Anika and all of his help in our alliance in the Wilds. I suddenly felt so selfish for not thinking of them over the last two days. Not even once.

Some empress I was.

I stepped out of the car as imperial guards shadowed behind me and I grabbed a handful of feathers from the basket at the entrance and held them in my hands. We believed that the sky and stars held the keys to our creation, and feathers from birds who lived in the sky would be our payment to the afterlife. Placing them in the graves was a sign of respect and payment to the creator to pass into eternity among the stars.

The people, amassed in the hundreds, made way for me, and I nodded to them as I passed. Half a dozen imperial soldiers flanked around me and Elaine. It was an eerie feeling to be among people and yet set apart from them. I didn't feel different, but my status said that I was. My father relished his title as emperor; he loved seeming above everyone. I hated it, and I wondered if I would ever grow used to it.

As I reached the first grave, a grief-stricken mother was bent on her knees before it, silent tears streaming down her face. The name *Mateo Braden* was carved into the headstone. I didn't know him. I should, but I didn't.

She looked up at me, and when I was fully confronted with the pain in her gaze, suddenly, war made no sense. They killed us. We killed them in retaliation. Back and forth until the end of time? I shook my head to dislodge the thoughts and then kissed my two fingers, touched the feather, and dropped it into the open grave. It slowly fluttered down onto the top of the maple-stained casket, landing among the dozens of other feathers.

The mother nodded at my show of respect. "Thank you," she whispered up at me.

I had no words for her; nothing was coming to me. *Thank you for your son's service? He died a hero? I'll get back at Luska in his honor and kill their sons?* They were empty sentiments, screaming into a void of pain and desperation.

Instead, I kneeled down and met her gaze head-on. "I'm sorry," I said earnestly.

She nodded, letting the tears fall freely, and then I stood.

I'm sorry. It was all I could offer. Two stupid words to mark the death of a healthy young man.

I moved to the next grave and the next, kissing my fingers and sending my blessing and well-wishes to the souls who had passed on their journey to the sky. Each dead body broke something in me. As the newly appointed leader, I took each one personally. Even as I grieved my own father, I also grieved these sons and daughters, mothers and fathers. When I was met with a family member, I could only offer them two words.

I'm sorry.

I felt like an imposter. My father would have handled this so much better. He would have given some speech about how these soldiers died heroes, and we would pay back Luska in kind, but I didn't have the strength for that. It was too sad, and I was grieving my own loss. I'd have to find it, though, because tonight, we would retaliate on Luska for what they did, and I'd need all the might I could muster then.

When I reached the final grave, I saw that it was Nikhil's headstone. Beside it, Kohen crouched next to his fallen best friend's grave, and my body went rigid. He peered up at me, and our gazes locked. Kohen's eyes were red-rimmed and my heart twisted in my chest. I wanted to stay with him, to take him into my arms and tell him everything would be okay, but I couldn't. Especially not after what he said last night.

I love you.

Saying those words had ruined everything. But I couldn't think about any of that now.

Gasps and murmurs rang throughout the space. I spun to see what the commotion was, just in time to see Liana descend from the sky.

I faced my creature as the crowd parted, and she stepped closer to me.

'I know your custom. Take one of my feathers for him,' she said.

My heart pinched at her offer. The feather of a firebird would surely get any soul into the afterlife.

I reached out and grasped one of her purple feathers that faded to orange at the tip and plucked it out. Kissing my fingers, I touched the feather and dropped it into Nikhil's grave. As it fell, it smoked and then turned to flames, eliciting a gasp from onlookers, including myself. By the time it touched his casket, it was powdery ash.

'May his soul live forever,' Liana said.

'Thank you,' I told her.

I peered over at Kohen. He gave me a thankful smile and a nod.

I wanted to tell him I was sorry like I had everyone else

who was grieving their lost loved ones, but I felt if I said anything to him, I might crack. Meeting his brothers, hearing him tell me he loved me and that I'd one day be his wife… it changed things between us. I felt like I was walking a path I could no longer turn back from, and it scared me.

I nodded back at him. Keeping things professional.

When I glanced back at the casket a final time, I noticed the ash pile where the feather had landed was shimmering purple and orange as it regrew. An eternal feather. Liana had given Nikhil something that would last forever, and it touched my heart.

I spied Anika off in the distance, and as the priest began his final prayers, I slipped away from the crowd and went over to her. She leaned against a tree, silent tears streaming down her face. I stood in front of her, saying nothing for a few moments. She was stuck in the throes of grief and probably survivor's guilt. They taught us about it in my training at the Imperial Academy. Experiencing war and having friends die left and right when only you remained wore on you after a while.

"It's not your fault," I said, and her face contorted into agony.

"It should have been me," she growled. I liked Anika. I'd tried not to, but the woman had grown on me. It killed me to see her like this.

I shook my head. "No. It should have been no one, but

fate took him, and we have to live on and do good things in his name."

Anika's tears evaporated in an instant, and her face drew into a snarl. "Tell me you're planning revenge on Luska for this attack?"

I gave her a small nod. "I am." I liked that Anika was treating me the same as any other day. She hadn't bowed or called me Empress or made me feel any different. She stepped away from the tree and closed the distance to within a foot of me. The guards to my left and right inched closer, but I put out my hand to stay them. Anika was no threat to me.

"Take me with you. Whenever the attack is, I want in." She lowered her voice. The wind stirred around us, and I knew it was a demonstration of her power. My gaze flicked to the woods at the edge of the cemetery to see her lioness lying in the grass, tail swishing as she watched me carefully.

I knew how Anika felt. I did. I wanted my own revenge for my father, and I wanted it firsthand. But the admirals would never approve her to go on the mission. She was a rookie and an Imbrian—two strikes against her. I had barely convinced them to allow Kohen.

"I can't do that. But I can promise you that justice for Nikhil will be dealt by the hand of an Imbrian." My gaze flicked to Kohen, and she relaxed a little, giving me a curt nod. That seemed good enough for her.

"Are you going to be posted at Sky Reach from now on?" she asked me.

Unease rolled down my spine. Why did she want to know? It was just like Elaine said. Until people were questioned by Admiral Caruso, I would trust no one.

I hated it when Elaine was right.

Anika must have taken my hesitation for what it was, mistrust, because she rolled her eyes.

"I didn't kill your father, Aisling. I'm only asking because I want to be posted there, too. We all do. Dev, Meera, Kian, Tetra. Even Alek and Roc. The alliance should stay together now more than ever." She seemed determined.

They had talked about staying together? Staying with me? That touched me.

Her words brought me back to my conversation with Elaine in the car. "I don't want anyone getting hurt." I shook my head, and Anika growled, causing my security detail to take another two steps forward, but I waved them off again.

Anika met my gaze. "I'm not a delicate flower, *Empress*." She said the word like it was dirty. "Your father was sending Meera, Kian, Dev, and I to be glorified security guards at the mines. Is that what you think of me? Of my potential?"

He was? I... hadn't known that. I should have asked him, but I had only been worried about Tetra and Kohen.

All of them had incredible powers. Why would he send them to keep the mines secure? Any old Fleet soldier could do that. One with a creature belonged at an army base. It was disrespectful. It was because they were Imbrian. It was wrong.

My father wasn't perfect; I knew that. He grew up in a time when Imbria was plotting takeovers and bombing our train stations. It was hard to breed that kind of thing out of someone. But times had changed.

"What about Thunder Cliff?" I asked her. "A badass base that gives you a better chance at survival."

She shook her head. "We want to be with Kohen *and* help protect you," she declared, and jealousy rushed through me at the way she said his name. There was an ache in her voice, and I knew at that moment that she knew Kohen and I were something. I wasn't sure what we were, but she knew. I hadn't even assigned Kohen to Sky Reach yet, but I guess that was inevitable, too.

"Empress," Elaine called behind me. It was time to go. I had to check in with my sisters and then start my flight to Sky Reach to speak with the admirals and initiate the attack on Luska. Elaine would have to leave right away and take the express train just to line up time with me. If all went well, I'd blow the Luskin Palace sky-high tonight.

"Okay, but if you die, the blood won't be on my hands. I warned you," I told Anika.

She grinned and bowed her head slightly. "Yes, Empress."

The way she said it was laced with some friendly sarcasm, and again, I found myself liking her. Anika was real.

Like Tetra. There wasn't an ounce of fake nice in her, and I respected the hell out of that.

"See you at Sky Reach, soldier," I told Anika.

She saluted me properly, respectfully, and I hoped to every star in the sky that I wouldn't regret this decision.

I prayed Kohen would forgive me for assigning everyone he loved to a suicide mission. Not many first years survived Sky Reach.

CHAPTER SIX

After checking in with my sisters and having lunch with them, I dealt with a few more matters of state, including getting this stupid cast off my arm, and then set out for Sky Reach. It was a three-hour flight through beautiful countryside, but my mind chewed on things the entire time. Did I make the right choices today? Firing Lucinda, assigning Tetra, Kohen, and all of our Wilds alliance to Sky Reach? Even Alek. I wanted to be with all my friends, but that felt selfish. Elaine double-checked with each one of them, and they all said they wanted to go to Sky Reach. We gave them the option to back out. No one did. Which made me respect them all more.

'Incoming,' Liana said, and I tensed, clenching my thighs onto her saddle and preparing to fight. *'Never mind, it's Onyx and Kohen,'* she said, relieved.

I relaxed, peering behind me, and saw nothing. I looked to the left and right, but all I saw were clouds.

"Up here!" Kohen called.

I peered up at the giant black dragon belly and smiled at Kohen, peeking over Onyx's side.

"I'm coming down!" he shouted down to me.

"What? No!" I screamed, but he had already slid one leg over and was dangling from the harness strap on Onyx.

"Are you insane! You could die!" I yelled as my heart leaped into my throat.

He dropped onto Liana's back right behind me and held on to my waist to steady himself.

"No, I've seen the future beyond this day, and I'm very much alive," he breathed against my ear.

My stomach warmed at the close contact, and I couldn't help but lean back into him. I turned my head to look him in the eyes.

"We can't do this. I'm sorry," I told him.

Our faces were inches from each other.

He nodded, leaning forward and taking my bottom lip into his mouth. I moaned, unable to tell him no because every fiber of my being was screaming "*Yes,*" including my heart. It was like today at the funeral we were strangers, but when we got alone, he was a different person. I kind of loved it.

"Kohen," I breathed as his palms flattened against my belly, tucking me even closer to him.

"Yes, my Empress?"

Those words held so much emotion. Loyalty, adoration, humility.

"If we get caught, they'll kill you, and I don't know what they will do to me," I told him.

"We won't get caught then." He said, and warmth bloomed in my gut as he peppered my neck with kisses.

I peered up into his eyes, trying to ferret out anything there that might show me that he wasn't serious. But all I saw were layers of pain mixed with passion. I tried to remind myself that he'd just buried his best friend today, and I'd be lying if I didn't admit that I loved his touch.

"If you're just looking to have sex, look elsewhere," I said boldly, my wound from Jace reopening at that moment.

He frowned, removing his hands from my belly. "Aisling, I'm in love with you. I would never—"

I gasped at the words, at how easily he said them. *Again*. "You don't love me," I told him incredulously. "You love some future version of me you've seen in your visions." I needed to fight this to get him to stop saying it.

He seemed to think about that for a minute. "Maybe. But I also love *this* version. The one that tries to push me away, the one who is so loyal to her best friend she partnered with her father's sworn enemy to keep her alive in the Wilds. The one who loves her sisters and almost slit my throat when she thought I had snuck into her house and harmed them. I love *this* version of you, too, Aisling, *and* all the others I've seen in the future."

His declaration tore my heart wide open. I'd loved Jace. I'd loved him with my whole heart, and he'd betrayed me. He cut me so deeply I was scared to ever love someone like that again. It was safer not to. I had to look out for myself now. But it was hard to deny Kohen. He was everything I never knew I needed.

Kohen's fingers stroked my neck. "I know you've been hurt." He grasped the bottom of my chin and pulled my lips to hover near his. "I only want what you're willing to give. And if you take it away at any moment, that's okay, too. I want you on your terms, Aisling."

It was the sexiest thing a man had ever said to me. Wanting me on my terms. Giving me permission to give whatever I had and also to take it away if I felt done. It was what I needed.

I whimpered, nodding, and pressed my lips to his, knowing that in my secret place, deep inside of myself that I shared with no one, I loved him too. But I'd never tell him. It would be cleaner that way when I cut things off to marry whoever Elaine and my advisors thought I should.

'We're getting close.' Liana broke my trance, and I pulled away from Kohen, panting.

Onyx hovered below us this time, and Kohen met my fiery gaze with one of his own, a half-cocked grin on his face. "I'm starting to see my gift as a blessing. I get to have you in my visions and then again in real life when the vision finally plays out." He planted one more soft, warm kiss on my lips. "Lucky me, to be able to have you twice."

My heart squeezed at that. Did that mean he'd had a vision about this right here? Before I could ask, he dropped down onto Onyx's back and flew ahead to Sky Reach.

I was equally excited and scared at the prospect of a secret relationship with him.

Liana cut into my thoughts: *'Be careful there, Aisling. You're empress now, and a lot of people will have an opinion on who you want to be with.'*

'Oh yeah, and how do you know that?' I asked her playfully. She wasn't wrong, but what did a creature of the Wilds know of such things?

She was quiet for a moment, and I sensed that I'd struck a chord with her.

'Remember I told you of my grandmother? That you two share the same gift?'

I tried not to think of *that* gift. Or curse. However you wanted to put it. The ability to control another's will felt too dangerous a power to have. Which is why if anyone ever found out, I'd be quickly and quietly killed.

I did remember when Liana told me about her grandmother. Thinking about her life from a time way back before she found herself here was too wild for my brain to ruminate on since it was thousands of years ago.

She was ancient.

'My grandmother was the empress of our people, and her council tried to control who she mated with. It didn't end well for any of them.'

My stomach dropped at that admission. *'Your grandmother, the one with the thrall, was an empress?'*

'We call our leader Tsarina, but yes. She was... maybe still is. I don't know.'

I frowned at that. *'That would make you... like a princess, or heir, or something?'*

I could sense her smile beneath me. *'It would. We are similar in that. Except you are empress now and no longer an heir.'*

This revelation was mind-blowing. The entire time I'd been with Liana, she never told me she was the empress' daughter, just like me! Sky Reach came into view, and I almost wanted to tell Liana to turn back for a bit and fly circles above the forest. I wanted to know more about her life. She never spoke of the past. I assumed it was too painful, so I never asked.

'If firebirds live forever, that means your grandmother could still be the leader, right? Or maybe it's your mother now, the Tsarina.' I tried the word out; the "t" was silent.

She was quiet so long I thought I had offended her and she wasn't going to answer me.

'My mother died during the Great Fall. Best not to think of these things now. They were a very, very long time ago. As you get

older, you will learn not to dwell on the past, Aisling. Living forever is painful that way.'

I wanted to know what the Great Fall was and more about her mother, like how could she die if female firebirds were immortal? But I knew then that it was too painful, so I said nothing more. Sometimes, when I probed my bond with Liana to sense where she was or how she was feeling, if I went a little too deeply, there was a dark cavern of sorrow there. She was hiding something from me, something horrific that she didn't want to remember or think back on. I respected that, and I didn't push.

We landed in the middle of the base next to Onyx just as Admiral Caruso grabbed Kohen by the upper arm and hauled him away, her creature trotting alongside them. The admiral's face wore signs of recently being mauled by a bear or something. Her left eye was swollen shut, her lip was split, and her cheeks were a sickly shade of greenish purple, marred with bruises.

My heart stopped in my chest, and my gaze flew to Elaine. Vespa stood tall beside her, the electric pink ember marks on her russet fur pulsing. A light rain began to fall as I slid off of Liana and walked briskly over to Elaine, my gaze tracking Kohen and the admiral as they stepped into a nondescript building at the back of the campus.

"What the hell is going on?" I asked, eyeing the place Kohen had just been dragged to in a manner that suggested he was in trouble.

Elaine peered at me like I was simpleminded. "You think I trust him around you and on this mission without clearing him of any wrongdoing with your father's death first?"

My heart restarted but thumped faster than ever before. If I was being honest, a very small part of me thought Kohen could have killed my father. He had motive, and he was there that night.

"He wouldn't do that," I said lamely because I wanted it to be true, especially after kissing just now. I wanted more kisses.

Elaine pinned me with a pointed look. "You don't know that, Aisling." There was suspicion in her gaze as if she were wondering why I would stick up for the Imbrian.

I glanced down at Elaine's knuckles to see they were purple and swollen.

"Did you do that to Caruso's face?" I asked, putting two and two together.

Pain crossed Elaine's features momentarily. "She's been cleared of any suspicion surrounding your father's death," was all she said. I knew then how hard that must have been for her, but it was good to know I was in the company of those I could trust.

She then inclined her head to the main war room building. "You have a lot of people waiting for you," she said and walked towards the building. I followed her with dread in my stomach.

Night had fallen. It was time to pay back Luska for what

they did to Riverine. But my mind was scattered now. What if Kohen *did* kill my father? What if this entire time, he'd wormed his way into my life just to get close to my father and take him down—and I was next? What if he wanted to take over all of Amersea and Imbria and rule both as king?

'If Kohen wanted you dead, you'd be dead by now. He's had many chances,' Liana said, and I took in a deep, cleansing breath. She was right. I hated myself for how quickly I mistrusted people now. Food tasters and round-the-clock security were making me paranoid.

My gaze flicked to the blue steel door Caruso had pulled Kohen into. I prayed to every star in the sky that he be cleared of any involvement. I couldn't handle that kind of betrayal—especially after Jace. I'd never trust a man again.

I stepped into the war room, and everyone saluted me. I strode over to the table, and we dove right into the plan. I was listening, but I was also eyeing the war room door. Why wasn't Kohen back yet with the admiral? How long did it take to ask one question? *Were you in any way involved in the death of the emperor?* Unless he was... and she was arresting him right now...

"My men spent all night building the payload," Commander Ledger said, pulling me back to reality. "It's big enough to take out the Red Palace but not too big that it will hurt any surrounding civilian buildings."

I nodded. "That's good." The War Code was important to me. Without them, we were monsters. Innocent casualties sometimes happened, but we did our best to avoid them at all costs. Although the Luskin people would probably slit my throat given the chance, I didn't blame them for the actions of their leader.

Some newcomers joined the meeting, and I was introduced to the other soldiers who would be riding with us on the mission. Lieutenant Colt, a tall and handsome twenty-five-year-old, would be going with me. The two that would be with Kohen were Sergeant Finn and Captain Jade. The female, Jade, who had long red hair, was bound to a wolf. Finn, a stocky, short-haired guy in his twenties, was bonded to a tiger. They were all a part of the elite squadron known as the Shadow Blades, named as such because they were rarely seen or heard until their blade was at your throat. These two men and one woman were the best assassins we had, and would be accompanying us in the off chance we made landfall, and I needed extraction. We were hoping to keep this all in the air, though, especially since only Colt had a creature of the air, a hawk. The other creatures obviously wouldn't be going with us on the mission.

Liana would fly us over the building, we would drop the payload, and fly home. That was the plan.

Five more minutes went by, and my palms started to sweat. Where was Kohen? He wouldn't kill my father... would he?

Of course he would! My father killed his dad—granted, that was in retaliation for the train attack, but Kohen had motive for such a thing. My heart started to beat so quickly that I felt a little dizzy. He said he loved me. I kissed him. Did I kiss my father's murderer? Nausea rolled through my gut. My gaze flicked to Elaine, who was watching the door as much as I was. What was taking them so long?

Elaine must have read my mind because she moved from the corner of the room to the door, probably to go check on him, just as it opened.

I nearly sagged against the wall when Kohen and Caruso stepped inside, chatting easily. She laughed at something he said, and I exhaled all the breath I hadn't realized I'd been holding.

Holy crap. I couldn't believe I had actually thought Kohen would kiss me one second and murder my father the next.

I gave a small laugh, and everyone looked at me, so I turned it into a throat-clearing.

"Shall we recap for Specialist Badshah so he is brought up to speed?" I asked. I was sure to use his newly minted rank, which hopefully sent a message to everyone in the room. He'd graduated, the same as I had. He was one of us. We were no longer cadets.

The high-ranking military officials in the room watched Kohen walk to the center of the table like they were watching a poisonous snake. Their eyes never left him as if they expected him to attack them all at any moment. I observed him with a different eye. My gaze ran the length of his tight t-shirt as I dreamed about touching what was under it.

Knowing that Caruso had cleared him of any involvement with my father's death made something click inside of me.

I trusted him, and I could count on two hands how many people in this world I trusted.

Trust was sexy, I had decided.

Kohen flicked me a little glance and came to join us at the war table. He stood next to me and moved his leg in such a way that it lay against mine as he leaned over the table to peer at the map and hear the game plan. We were all crammed in this room, over fifteen of us, so no one looking might think anything of it, but I felt the intention behind his touch. His deliberate way of touching me made me also harken to the words he'd uttered to me.

I love you.

What a crazy fool.

Love? It was for puppies. My father was right. Loving Jace got me nowhere. I loved my family. I loved Elaine and Tetra. But loving Kohen wasn't going to happen. I couldn't let it, or if it had already happened, I couldn't acknowledge it. I wasn't sure I'd survive it when he was ripped away from me, and I was forced to marry someone else to appease the people. No, love wasn't on the menu.

"Ready, Empress?" someone asked, and I jerked my head in that direction, slowly pulling my leg away from Kohen's, and nodded. "Let's do this."

Tonight was about revenge for my father. I needed to focus on that and not the burning desire Kohen had lit inside of me. Because I felt like I could burn the whole world down with this heat currently resting over me.

Kohen met my gaze, and I quickly looked away. I didn't trust myself not to moan right here in front of everyone just by him looking at me.

"Let's show Luska what happens when they mess with our capital," I told the room.

The men and women present broke into roars of agreement, and we stepped outside and readied for our mission.

I was confident all would go well, with little issue, since Kohen said that he saw us hit our target in his vision.

Boy, was I wrong.

CHAPTER SEVEN

I'd never been this deep into Luska before. It was breathtakingly beautiful. Snowcapped mountains surrounded most of the northern border in the distance, and the moon above us lit up a lush green landscape filled with farms and gardens. We passed a decent stretch of the Wilds where the fire sky above it trickled ember down onto the land.

The Luskins bonded with a lot of Talanagi, so that meant they would have flyers too: dragons, griffins, and all the like. I kept my eyes peeled to the skies, but they probably didn't expect a sky attack from us. Amerseans didn't have Talanagi until Kohen and I came along, which gave us an advantage.

Kohen and I flew about two hundred feet apart so that we didn't draw attention moving so closely together. Liana had been fitted with a special two-person saddle, and Lieutenant Colt sat behind me as his hawk creature flew alongside us. Onyx and Liana were in constant mental communication, and we were all well-versed in the plan. I'd expected to be more nervous but I wasn't. I was in enemy territory, about to carry out a revenge plot so grand that if we succeeded, it would go down in history books. My father would not die in vain.

We moved under the cover of night for two reasons. One, it would conceal us, and two, so the Red Palace would be empty of tourists, occupied by only a few soldiers who guarded the perimeter. I wasn't trying to kill a bunch of innocent Luskins; I was trying to make a statement. You kill my father... You attack our training center for imperial soldiers... I take out the one place you hold dear.

The Red Palace was Luska's pride and joy, a masterpiece of architecture with spires and arches painted in red and gold that would make your jaw drop. I'd seen paintings of it over the years of my schooling. It also held all of their parliament meetings and war councils and some famous artwork they revered. But most importantly, it was the office of Prime Leader Vlek. We had little intel on the man. We didn't know where he lived or how many children he had. But we knew from an Imperial Fleet prisoner who had broken free that Vlek worked in this building and that they held daily tours open to the public, including schoolchildren. Taking out his office at night would send a message to the people of Luska.

You are not invincible, and you're going to pay for what you did to my father. But I wasn't a monster and wouldn't hurt children.

I peered down at the payload clutched between my creature's claws, an explosive made of some of the most powerful dynamite we had in Amersea. This thing could blow the side off of a mountain. Dropped directly into the center courtyard of the Red Palace, it would flatten the structure completely.

'Kohen says that when we get close, we will have to act quickly lest we be spotted by guards. He will wait for your command.'

I sent her my acknowledgment through the bond as we headed due north. We were getting close now. I could see some lights of the city still on. It was late, just past midnight, so most people would be asleep. I hoped my father was among the stars, looking down on me with pride. I wouldn't let Luska get away with what they'd done. For Nikhil and everyone else who'd died, we'd get revenge.

I peered down at the city as Liana began her descent and spotted the giant red building on the horizon. It was all lit up, floodlights beaming on their pride and joy, and for a moment, I ached to ruin such a masterpiece.

As we got lower and grew closer, I had to admit it was more beautiful than the pictures. Every inch of the building had some piece of hand-painted art, a pattern of swirls, a man blowing a trumpet, a soldier flying a creature. All painted in red and gold, it was breathtaking.

'Now or never!' Liana cried. We were about to be directly

over the center courtyard. I peered below to see two guards dressed in their red uniforms patrolling the space with their creatures behind them. I didn't relish taking a life, but I thought of all of the lives they'd taken from us, how they wouldn't stop until our lands were expunged of Amerseans and they'd stolen all of our ember.

I gave the command: *'Drop it.'*

Liana released her claws and the payload dropped like a rock just as she veered to the right and out of harm's way. Kohen and Onyx veered with us, and moments later the bomb ignited, sending a shockwave through the sky so powerful it rattled my chest.

It happened too fast. I gave the order and it happened. It was done.

"Holy stars!" Lieutenant Colt said from where he perched behind me. I'd forgotten he was even here. I was so lost in my thoughts.

I peered over my shoulder to see the most magnificent explosion I'd ever laid eyes on. A ball of fire reached for the sky; the bricks of the building were blowing outward in all directions. The structure was torn apart and then collapsed in on itself in seconds.

Kohen and I both grinned at each other, thrusting our fists in the air. We did it. We'd brought down the freaking Red Palace of Luska! Something even my father couldn't achieve in his time. The thrill quickly fled as I felt Liana tense beneath me.

'Incoming.'

I craned my neck to see a shadow bolt across the sky.

It was a dragon with a rider; I could tell by the wings.

Liana inhaled through her nose and tensed even further. Smoke leaked from her nostrils in long white tendrils, and she glanced up at me with flaming yellow eyes.

'Permission to seek revenge for my mate,' she asked, and a shock went through me.

What did she just say?

Our escape plan was to fly east and then head south, low over the Wilds until we hit the Wall. Liana increased her speed, super-fast, aiming east as she began to descend over the Wilds of Luska, which they called the Forbidden.

'What do you mean revenge for your mate?' I asked her, casting worried glances over my shoulder as Colt pulled a bow. The shadow of the dragon was in the distance now.

That's when I was hit with a montage of images that flashed from Liana's mind into mine.

Her mate, Aldan, a male firebird with black and blue feathers that faded to white, had died protecting her from the very dragon that was in the sky chasing us right now. Liana had been in a vulnerable position at the time, wounded and healing from a territorial battle, when Drak, the alpha dragon behind us, took out her mate. Normally, Liana protected her mate in such battles since she had an infinite lifespan. Aldan was a powerful fighter, but he was not immortal. But that time, she could not.

My chest heaved, and I fought to keep from sobbing as Liana replayed Aldan's final moments to me in vivid detail.

Drak, a green dragon, ripped Aldan's throat out right in front of an injured Liana. She was so heartbroken that she burst into flames and died right then and there, but Drak, being impervious to flame, was uninjured.

The images stopped, and Liana landed on the ground inside of the Forbidden.

"Why are we landing here?" Lieutenant Colt hissed from behind me.

"Get off," I growled at him, unable to contain my rage at Drak. He did as ordered.

Liana had waited years to see the green dragon again. Tonight we would get revenge, not just for my father, but for her mate as well.

'You understand why I have to do this?' Liana asked me.

'Of course. Permission granted. Let's cut him into a thousand pieces,' I declared and pulled my blade.

Liana sighed.

Forgive me, Aisling,' she said, and then she bucked me. I went flying, a scream of surprise ripping from my throat as I dropped the blade so that I didn't accidentally stab myself with it. I hit the forest floor hard, landing on my shoulder just as Liana kicked off and took to the sky.

'No!' I shouted after her.

'I would never be able to live with myself if you got hurt,' she shared.

'He's dangerous. You need my help!' I shrieked as I scrambled to stand.

I'd just learned that Drak was an alpha dragon, which meant he was very powerful—stronger and faster than any other male Talanagi. His power was something she was hiding from me. It scared her.

'I'm immortal. You might not be. We do not know,' Liana said as she pumped her wings higher and higher. *'And I have help. Onyx is with me.'*

A second shadow joined her side, and I recognized the black dragon as Onyx. But there was no rider on him.

Kohen? Finn, Jade?

A twig snapped behind us and both Lieutenant Colt and I spun.

I relaxed when I recognized Kohen and the two other special-ops soldiers.

Kohen looked pissed. "Onyx kicked us off for some suicide mission against a rival dragon."

I pursed my lips. "That rival dragon killed Liana's mate."

Kohen nodded. "And Onyx's parents. I know. But I want to help."

I shook my head. "We can't." I peered up at the sky and the two fading figures. "We can't fly without them."

"What the hell is going on here?" Jade looked winded. A few leaves were tucked into her long red hair, and her entire left side was covered in dirt. It seemed they got bucked off in a hurry, too.

I sighed. "It's complicated. Can you give us a minute?"

Jade nodded, pulling out her map. "I'll plot us a course home."

The three of them walked away about twenty paces to a flat rock where they could spread their maps, giving Kohen and me some privacy. They began to speak in hushed tones about a way back when Kohen frowned. He was clearly still upset we were not helping Liana and Onyx.

Moving closer to Kohen so that we could not possibly be overheard, I leaned into him. "Kohen, did you see this? How this will end?" I whispered.

He glanced down at my lips and moaned a little. "Stars, I want to kiss you right now," he whispered back.

I smacked his chest hard, and he caught my fingers, stroking my palm with his fingers. "Focus," I chastised him but secretly loved that he was seemingly infatuated with me. Knowing Caruso had interrogated him with her power and found him innocent had made me care all the more for him, trust him all the more.

"So long as those lips are attached to that face, I will never focus again," he said.

Damn. His smooth talking got me hook, line, and sinker. I couldn't help but grin.

"Have you seen our creatures die or anything horrible?" I asked him.

He shook his head. "In the future, you ride Liana, and I ride Onyx. Same as always."

I relaxed at that. "So this will probably be okay?"

He shrugged. "Probably."

He was still holding my fingers, so I pulled them back to my chest before the others could see.

"Except..." he added with a wince, and my whole body tensed.

"Except what?" I asked.

"I mean, I have visions where Liana isn't around you... Is she dead or just off hunting...? I don't know."

My mouth went dry. "Well, if she dies, she can rebirth," I whispered because that wasn't something I liked to advertise.

He nodded. "But she could be held captive or tortured..."

"Kohen!" I hissed.

"I'm sorry. I'm just learning that glimpsing snippets of the future doesn't always make sense in moments like this."

I scoffed. "Like when you supposedly glimpsed me as your wife."

It flew out of my mouth before I could take it back.

He went very still. "I shouldn't have told you that. I don't want that stuff to interfere with the natural progression of our relationship."

Relationship? We were in a relationship? Why did that excite me?

"Too late, Kohen, especially for you," I told him. If he really did see our future, then he knew everything about where this would lead.

He grinned then, and it made my knees weak. This man had become my weakness, which my father would not have tolerated. Which *I* shouldn't tolerate.

"I was a goner the moment I laid eyes on you, Aisling," he confessed.

That was before he got his future sight gift. That was all the way at the Lottery.

"Empress?" one of the soldiers asked, and I took two huge steps away from Kohen.

Focus, Aisling, you're the leader of the largest country in the world.

I spun. "Yes, Lieutenant."

"We think that if we head—" Colt stopped and cocked his head to the side as if speaking to his creature. The hawk flew down from the sky and landed off to the side, perching on the top branches of a tree directly to our right.

"My creature says that there are over a dozen flying Talanagi circling the skies now. She's going to stay low so that we aren't found. They will send out ground troops soon to—"

He gasped just as I saw something blue move to our right, where his hawk was perched. I pulled my father's sword just as a griffin leaped down from where it must have been hiding in the thick branches of the tree and gobbled Colt's hawk into its mouth. One second, his creature was perched on a branch, and the next, she was... *eaten.*

The griffin cocked its head to the side and peered down

at us with one of Colt's hawk's tail feathers still poking out of his mouth. My heart broke as Colt let out a silent wail. It was the most soul-crushing thing I'd ever seen. The soldier opened his mouth to scream but knew he couldn't attract anyone right now, so he just shook with rage as agony contorted his face.

The griffin leaped from the tree and landed before us, cocking its head to the side.

Kohen pulled his blade, stepping in front of me protectively. Finn and Jade did the same. But the griffin didn't seem to have any interest in me. He was staring right at Colt.

It was horrifying. One moment to have your creature alive and well, and the next... gone. Murdered.

There was no human jumping out of the thick woods to attack us.

"I think he's unbonded," I breathed, feeling crushed after witnessing what had just happened. The Wilds were brutal in that way. We needed to get out of here.

I knew they called them the Shadow Blades for a reason, but I'd never seen them in action until now. One second Colt was standing with unbridled rage, fists shaking as he clenched his jaw, and then in a blink he had pulled his knife and thrown it into the griffin's wing. The blade sank into flesh and the griffin shrieked, staggering backward, and I swallowed hard. We all took a step back, and in another blink, Colt was at the griffin's throat with a second blade. He was incredibly fast, but before he could slice into the creature, the griffin made a clicking noise with his tongue and then we were all flying backward. Some kind of shock-wave had emitted from the creature. My butt hit the ground first as Kohen threw himself over me, pinning me to the ground.

Colt gave a battle cry, clearly no longer caring about making noise, and ran at the creature. Somehow, he'd pulled out a cord and lassoed it around the beast's neck. Then he was on the creature's back, pulling the cord tight to choke him. It was an incredible sight, and as much as I knew we should get away and move to safety, I couldn't stop watching the battle before me. Another clicking sound reached my ears and another shockwave shot out from the creature, this one rattling my lungs, but Kohen seemed to take the brunt of it since he was lying on top of me. Trees shook, but Lieutenant Colt stayed on him. The griffin kicked off the ground in a panic, and they both went skyward.

Holy crap.

I understood the desire to retaliate for his dead bonded, but right now was the worst possible time for this. There were over a dozen Talanagi in the skies. Colt was going to be seen.

"We need to get the empress to safety," Kohen said, standing.

Seargent Finn and Captain Jade eyed the sky where their friend had just gone and only hesitated about leaving him behind for a brief moment. "Of course," they said, and then I was yanked to my feet, and we were all running. Kohen, Finn, and Jade created a circle of protection around me.

I knew the motto. No man left behind.

"We should stay and wait for Lieutenant Colt." I slowed my pace, trying to wrap my head around how this had gone south so fast. We'd lost our creatures, and now Colt's hawk was dead and he was riding an unbonded creature into the sky on the night we blew up the Red Palace. If he was caught, the Luskins would torture him to death.

All three of the soldiers shook their heads. "That's not protocol when protecting you, Empress," Jade said as her long, red ponytail bobbed behind her. "We leave him. We can send an extraction team at another time if he survives." I could hear the quiver in her voice, though. She didn't like the rules.

If he survives.

I hated that. I did. But she was right. If Liana were with me, I'd fly up and help him take down the griffin. What could we do staring up at the sky? He was on his own.

"Let's head south and take the river around the Wall. I've done it before," Kohen stated and got a few raised eyebrows. I knew he'd done it before because I'd gone with him during our time together in The Wilds.

There was no argument, though. By Jade's calculations, it would take roughly two hours jogging on foot as we were pretty deep into Luska and far from the border, but travel on foot was our only option. We agreed that if we got split up, we'd meet on the other side of the Wall in the Wilds in Amersea. We'd run as fast and far as we could without stopping until we were out of enemy territory.

As we ran, my mind was with Liana and Onyx. Were they okay? I couldn't sense her at all—she'd completely shut me out. I wanted to reach out to her mentally, but I also didn't want to distract her if she was in a fight for her life.

I knew how important it was for her to get retribution for her mate, how long she'd waited to see Drak again. I just couldn't believe it was happening on the night that we took down the Red Palace. I also couldn't believe she'd left me behind. It hurt, even though I knew it was out of protection.

After about thirty minutes of solid running, I slowed, trying to catch my breath. The others matched my pace. I had a stitch in my side, so I grabbed it, pinching hard as I turned our run into a slow jog. No one questioned it. They just slowed to match me and kept their eyes peeled on the forest. The pain in my side eased, and I was about to say that we could run full-out again when Jade suddenly stopped, holding up a fist. The sign meant *pause and be alert.*

We all froze, and I heard it: the snap of a twig to our right.

Ever so carefully, I reached up to pull my blade and held out my free palm with the other. Kohen did the same, and fire began to build his palm as he suspended it there, waiting to attack.

It could just be another unbonded creature. We were in the Wilds, so it was teeming with them.

Jade moved then, tucking herself into a roll and hitting the ground just as a knife whizzed past where she was.

"Get her out of here!" Jade yelled and popped up, running into the woods as Kohen shot a ball of fire in the direction of where the knife had come from.

My heart hammered in my chest at the sight of Captain Jade disappearing into the forest. Kohen and Finn were now the only two left. They each hooked a hand under my elbow and guided me into a thick outcrop of trees. We ran in complete silence, other than the sound of our shoes pounding on the forest floor. A mere hundred feet away from us, I could hear Jade fighting an unseen intruder. Grunts, metal clangs, and fists hitting skin reached my ears, but we kept moving southeast. It felt wrong to run away from a fight, but I was empress now. If I was killed, it made Valor empress at fourteen. That was unheard of. There were protocols in place for a young heir, but they were less than ideal. Valor was still reeling from my father's death. She wasn't ready for this.

No, we had to keep going.

Jade knew what she signed up for. But even as I said it, I wondered if I could sneak away and help her. To use the thrall to subdue her attacker.

Yeah, right.

Then Jade would tell the Imperial Fleet, and I'd be hanging from a tree by morning.

I shook my head to dislodge the wild thoughts running through it. The mission had been a success, which was great, but I was naïve to think that we'd all just get home safely.

As the moments ticked by, we ran in the eerie pinkish-orange light the fire sky gave off. We were completely silent, slowly inching our way towards the Wall. It was all going according to plan when the breath was suddenly taken from my lungs. My lungs cinched in my chest, and I clawed at my throat as panic washed over me.

Red dragon rider.

I heard Kohen and Finn sputter for breath. We all skidded to a stop and faced each other. They beat on their chests in confusion, and I glanced upward, watching the red dragon circle above us. The Luskin rider with the blonde hair peered down at me, hovering twenty feet above, wearing a sadistic grin.

Without Liana or Onyx, we couldn't reach her.

Panic seized me as I found my lungs frozen, and Kohen peered at me with alarm. He aimed a fireball at her, but she dodged it easily, laughing as she coasted to the right on her dragon.

Finn threw a blade up at her, but it didn't reach, and I knew what needed to be done. We couldn't run away, not without oxygen. She was forcing me to use my hidden power.

I'd done it before in front of her. Maybe she wasn't sure and wanted to see me do it again. Either way, she was surely toying with us.

"This is for killing my father," she screamed down at me, lowering herself a little more, but still out of reach.

Her father? I didn't know who her father was.

Finn fell to his knees. Black dots danced at the edges of my vision. I didn't want to do this. I glanced at Kohen, whose lips were purple, and he just nodded to me once.

Dammit.

Pulling for that power within me, I threw out my hand. *'Stop!'* I thought, but never said out loud. The word was an action, and it flew from me in a physical force. The silver cord soared from my hand and wrapped around the red rider's head. Precious oxygen returned to our lungs as we gasped for air.

"I knew it!" she said as she peered down at me with wonder.

"I'm not done," I growled between ragged breaths. "Jump," I said, out loud this time, pushing my power. A little white glowing bead ran the length of the cord and rushed into her. She shook her head in panic, rearing her dragon to escape, but once the bead hit her head, she leaped off of her dragon and landed on both legs. From thirty feet away, I heard the bones snap. Her wails of agony cut into the night.

"That was for *my* father, for Nikhil, for all of Riverine," I told her.

"Holy shit!" Finn screamed. "You can... you just... that's *forbidden*."

Oh crap. What was I thinking?

I snapped my head in Finn's direction at the same time Kohen lunged for him.

Finn was wide-eyed, pale, and ashen. He ran, and Kohen took off after him.

No. No. No. I did not think that through. Finn seeing me use that power could ruin everything.

Without a second thought, I left the red dragon rider and ran after Kohen. The cord connecting me to the rider snapped and sucked back into me as we pounded through the woods.

"Seargent Finn! Stop! That's an order!" I yelled, watching him fly through the trees in a blind panic. He didn't stop, which meant he feared me and was no longer loyal. He'd tell everyone what I could do, and then I'd be—

Kohen threw a fireball at Finn's retreating back and it crashed into him, knocking him forward, covering him in flames.

I skidded to a stop, in shock at what Kohen had just done. Finn screamed a horrible shrill of pain as Kohen pulled his knife from the sheath at his side and ended Finn's agony quickly by dragging it across his neck.

No. No. No.

Kohen had just killed one of our own in order to protect my secret. I stood there in shock as Kohen wiped the blood off his blade, sheathed it, and came to stand before me. He reached for me and I tensed, so he withdrew.

"Aisling, if you hadn't used your power, we'd all be dead," he said.

I knew that. But did I need to make the dragon rider jump off? Break her legs? And maybe her back. *She killed Nikhil.* What was I thinking? Of course, I didn't care what happened to her. It felt like I was going insane, a war going on inside my own mind.

I looked at Finn's smoking, lifeless body. "But he was one of us," I croaked, feeling on the edge of losing it. Too much death, too close together, too fast. I needed to process it, and I needed more sleep.

Kohen shook his head, and this time, pulled me into his arms. I let him. He cradled my jaw and forced me to look at him.

"My love, it will always just be you and me, not us and them."

Those words sounded romantic in a way, but I knew he didn't mean them to be. He meant it was he and I who knew about my gift, and then everyone else. Us against the world.

"The red dragon rider knows," I told him.

He nodded. "Let her. If she lives, she will take that information back to Prime Leader Vlek. He will fear you. It might end the war. You could force him to surrender."

I could? Why hadn't I thought that? Why didn't I *do* that?

"But only for a little while. We don't know how long your powers last," he added.

True. When I lost concentration, they broke. I couldn't end the war forever, but I could change it drastically.

"What do we do?" I looked at Finn's dead body, feeling a tidal wave of guilt wash over me. I was supposed to protect him, I was his empress, and I'd just led him to his death.

"We go to the meetup spot and see if Jade is there—"

"And if she is?" I asked, unable to tear my gaze away from Finn's dead, still-smoking body.

Kohen directed my chin so that I met his eyes again, and I finally looked away. "Aisling, he didn't follow your command. He would have told Commander Ledger, and you'd be put to death."

I knew that was true. I *knew* that, but... it didn't make it any easier to take. How many people had Kohen and I secretly killed together? First, the imperial soldiers in the Wilds, then the ones who were holding Liana hostage and keeping us from bonding. Now... this. It was too much.

"If we see Jade, we tell her of the red dragon rider. Finn died a hero trying to save you," Kohen declared.

I nodded. That was a good cover story, and his family would get extra pay for him dying in battle. "Okay..."

I needed Liana. I couldn't process this. I needed to know more about my gift, the one her grandmother had. I didn't want it anymore. I wanted to give it back.

"I wish I didn't have my power," I told Kohen.

He nodded, chewing at his lip and peering down at me anxiously.

"What? I asked.

He said nothing, but there was a look of compassion in his gaze.

"Kohen Badshah," I warned. He'd seen something. Some vision related to my power?

"You don't always have this power, Aisling," he said sadly, stroking my cheek.

Fear washed over me, fast and hot. "What do you mean? How?"

"I just know that you lose it, that there is a time you need it, and it doesn't come to you—for a short time or forever, I have no idea." He shrugged. "I wish I could fit all the puzzle pieces together, Aisling, I really do. But there are so many holes." I could see the agony written on his face as he tried to recall things in his mind, and I nodded, appreciating that he was being honest and sharing.

"When I really need it and don't have it... what happens to me?" I asked, suddenly fearful. This power felt like a curse, but not when it was saving my life.

His face became fierce. "Nothing you need to worry about because I will always protect you."

My heart fluttered. Kohen's loyalty and protectiveness and adoration was... overwhelming in the best way. I'd never sought safety from anyone, not even my father. I'd been taught to fend for myself, but with Kohen, I felt like I could lean on him and trust him to carry me through hard things.

He reached up and brushed his thumb over my bottom lip. "There's so much I want to say, Aisling, but I can't."

I swallowed hard, tendrils of heat rushing down my body at his touch. I wanted to hear all of the things he wanted to tell me, but I also knew that him speaking about the future before had freaked me out. About us. I wanted to live it, not hear about it and wonder if he was guiding me into it.

"Do we ever fight? Or are we blissfully happy forever?" I smiled up at him.

A dark shadow crossed over his face, and he eyed the tree line behind me. "Come on, we should get going." His hand slipped into mine and he pulled me forward, towards the Wall, but my mind was spinning. Why didn't he answer me? And why did I care so much?

Oh Kohen. He might be my undoing.

CHAPTER EIGHT

We finally made it to the Wall and then trudged through the river like we had in the Wilds right before we'd claimed Onyx and Liana. Kohen's warm hand in mine felt so natural that I'd forgotten we were even holding hands until the moment we stepped up to the Amersea border. He pulled his fingers from mine and offered for me to climb the riverbank first.

"After you, Empress," he said formally.

We were back in Amersea, back to hiding our relationship or whatever this was.

My mind raced with everything that had just happened. We blew up the Red Palace, Liana and Onyx left us, and then the red rider saw me use my power! Now Finn was gone. Oh stars, Kohen killed Finn just to keep my secret. I felt sick, like a delayed processing. The image of his burned skin was embedded into my mind and kept coming up when I thought of him.

Lieutenant Colt and Captain Jade were missing. This mission would be deemed a success in most eyes, but in mine, it had completely failed. I'd failed my people.

The second we stepped onto land, there was a rustle in the bushes to our right. I pulled my blade just as Jade stepped out, covered in mud and soaking wet.

"Empress." She bowed.

There was a bleeding cut above her left eyelid, but other than that, she looked okay.

Relief surged through me. She made it.

Her gaze peered behind Kohen and I, and my heart sank, crushing the sudden relief I'd felt.

"Finn?" Her voice shook, but she kept her cool. I had a feeling Finn, Colt, and Jade were all very close. I wanted to crawl into a black pit and hide forever.

Kohen bowed his head and placed his fist over his chest. "Died at the hands of a Luskin. Saved our empress' life."

The lie felt dirty, and guilt threatened to eat me alive, but Jade smiled. "A hero's death is all he ever wanted."

My gaze flicked to Kohen to see if any remorse or guilt shone there, but he was a mask of calm.

Remember, everything I do, I do to protect you, he'd once said to me. It was true. A harsh truth I was now living.

Jade stepped up before me and bowed deeply. "Now that you are back safely, I would like permission to go after Colt."

My father warned me of this. Decision fatigue. Being empress was like being shot with a dozen arrows every second, and you had to catch every single one. Except the arrows were decisions you had to make. I couldn't properly think about Liana, or Onyx, or the Red Palace, or even Finn. That was all in the past, and right now, I had to make another decision.

I wanted to tell Jade yes. I did. But a solo mission to go after someone last seen dangling from a Talanagi was suicide. Especially after we'd just bombed the Red Palace. No, we'd need to hunker down and get ready for a counterattack.

"Denied. Let's get back to base. We can plan Colt's rescue and extraction in the morning," I told her. "We need to brace for retaliation."

She hesitated a second as if she wanted to argue with me but then nodded, and we moved out. It took us a while to make it out of the Wilds, but when we did, there were over a dozen vehicles waiting for us. Jade had called them in through her creature, Danowen, who was waiting at base and had the gift of being able to mentally relay messages to anyone.

"What happened?" Commander Ledger asked. "All we knew from Danowen was that the building blew sky high, and then the empress was left behind by her creatures and attacked."

I gave him a quick debrief as we got into the car. His face

lit up at the confirmation that we'd completely flattened the Red Palace. I said that we'd been separated from our creatures in battle because I didn't want him to know we weren't exactly fully in control of Liana and Onyx. I would never force her to do anything. I told him exactly what Kohen said about Finn dying to protect me and that Colt was missing in action.

He nodded, and we traveled full speed back to base. "They'll retaliate. We should all spend the night in the underground bunkers."

I nodded. Sky Reach was constantly under fire. An elaborate maze of bunkers had been built to withstand attacks.

Within the hour I was ferried to a lavish sleep quarters fifty feet underground. As I descended all the steps, it felt like a tomb, but I tried to focus on the fact that it meant I was safe. Kohen and the rest of the base occupants would be sharing bunk beds. I was sequestered in a private suite that felt cold and lonely after growing up with three sisters. But I was too tired to care.

'Liana, tell me you're safe,' I called through our bond. But got nothing. I tried not to let it bother me. She was immortal after all, but I didn't like being separated from her.

I showered quickly, and the second my head hit the pillow, I was out.

I WAS RIPPED from a blissful sleep by a fist banging on my steel door. It felt like pulling my body from quicksand as I crossed the room and ripped the door open.

Commander Ledger was half asleep as well, hair flattened to one side and still wearing his bedclothes. "We have an urgent update that cannot be read without you present. Top-level clearance. Empress only."

I shook myself, adrenaline forcing alertness to unfoggy my mind. *Top clearance. Empress only.* That was bad. Or good. I wasn't sure. I hadn't gotten to that level of training with my father yet.

I threw a baggy sweater over my tank top and followed him down the hall, noticing he had only one sock on. I'd never seen this man look disheveled. He was always put together, always tidy. This must be serious to have him presenting himself to me like this. I smoothed my hair as we walked, retying my braid and wiping my eyes. Was I about to walk into a room full of people looking like this? Would I ever sleep a full night again?

We reached a door where a soldier stood out front, back erect, staring straight into the distance. As we approached, he simply glanced at us and then opened the door. I stepped inside, not sure what to expect.

It was a small, dimly lit room with an envelope sitting in the center of a table and white gloves beside it. There were four chairs, all empty.

It was just Commander Ledger and I.

Interesting.

My heart beat furiously in my chest as I stared at the cursive font on the letter.

Empress Aisling.

"Who is it from?" I asked.

"It came via Luskin currier."

Luska sent me a letter? I was pretty sure that was unheard of, but what did I know?

"Do they do this often?"

"Never," the commander said flatly. "Wear the gloves. We don't know if the paper is poisoned."

Great.

I reached for the gloves, proud to see that my hands didn't shake. Putting them on, I then grasped the letter and peeled off the back seal.

Commander Ledger paced the carpet as I pulled out a single note and read.

Empress Aisling,

Tonight, your attack on our Red Palace killed my father, Prime Leader Vlek—

I STOPPED READING, shock rushing through me. Holy crap. What did he just say? I killed the leader of the most war-hungry nation known to man?

"Prime Leader Vlek is dead from the attack," I announced in a hollow voice, and Commander Ledger stopped pacing. He turned to me with a sadistic grin and whooped a fist into the air.

"Hang on," I told him. "I haven't finished."

I've waited two decades to take over the war efforts from my weak father. So, I wanted to say thank you for giving me this wonderful opportunity. I'm going to give you two options now, and I'd like you to choose very carefully.

1. Marry me, unite our people, surrender your country, lands, and ember to me, and I will not harm anything you hold dear, including your three beautiful sisters.

MY HANDS SHOOK as I read the threat between his words. Marry him! Was he insane? I didn't even know Prime Leader Vlek had a son, or any children for that matter. I assumed so, as having heirs was smart, but if I didn't know much about him, how did he know so much about my sisters? I read on:

2. Deny my hand, and I'll strip your lands of their people, mine all of your ember, and kill each and every one of your sisters before forcing you to be my wife.

I await your reply,
Maxim

My skin began to smoke with barely contained rage.

"What did it say?" The commander peered up at me with alarm, glancing at the smoke rising off of my body.

I set down the letter on the table so he could read it and took in three deep, calming breaths in the hopes that my skin would stop smoking. Marry him? Not gonna happen.

And too bad for him, he'd done the one thing I'd never show any mercy for. He'd threatened to kill my sisters. How did he know so much about me? I didn't like that at all.

After reading the letter, Commander Ledger rubbed his jaw. "Vlek must have been working late in the building. That part is good news."

"How does he know about my sisters?" I asked.

He sighed. "They have Talanagi. They could send spies over in the night and fly out by morning, and we wouldn't know."

We watched the skies pretty closely because we knew they had a lot of fliers, but maybe not close enough.

That was unnerving, but he was right. Look how we'd just flown into Luska unnoticed.

"What do we know about Vlek?" I asked the commander.

Commander Ledger winced. "We heard he had a daughter. I didn't know about a son."

We had been asleep for decades when we could have sent in spies to ferret out all the intel on this family. Now I was going to have to pick up where my father lacked.

"I want more eyes on the sky. I want reinforced borders around Riverine, and I want to send a team of spies to find out more about this Maxim," I told him.

He nodded.

"And I want to send a reply," I said.

The commander bristled. "What kind of reply? We should bring this to the admirals to formulate a response together."

"The admirals have no say in who I marry." Which I was ninety-eight percent sure was true.

"Well, then, let me talk this out with you. I have some thoughts—"

"Get me Lieutenant Elaine Steele."

His brows bunched together. "Your governess? You want to bring a nanny in on the only written communication we've received from Luska in decades!"

"A nanny?" My voice was cold as I stalked over to him, walking right up into his face.

He swallowed hard, suddenly realizing that he'd overstepped. "I only meant that Lieutenant Steele is out of practice in matters of—"

"Out of practice!" I tipped my head back and laughed in his face. "The empress who stands before you, the one who just killed Prime Leader Vlek and leveled their palace, was *created* by Elaine Steele. Never forget that!" I snapped.

He lowered his gaze and nodded. "Yes, Empress. But imperial law states that in order for Lieutenant Steele to read that letter, she'd have to be an admiral or higher."

I nodded in understanding. "Then make her an admiral. I'll wait."

I walked over to a desk, grabbed a piece of paper and pen, and then looked over at him.

His mouth opened in shock. "Oh, you're serious?"

"Yes," I said plainly.

"I advise against that. The admiral title is—"

"Noted. Now, are you going to do as I have asked, or will I have to demote you and find someone else who can follow orders?"

A mask of anger crossed his face, but I held firm. He would always see me as the little kid who dated his son if I didn't show him who I really was—that if you peeled back my skin, you'd find steel and concrete. I wasn't soft, and he couldn't intimidate me.

"Yes, Empress." He saluted me and left the room.

Ten minutes later, Elaine stepped into the room with her hair in a messy bun and wearing a black robe. She was alone and wide-eyed as she stared at the note on the table, unable to read it from where she stood.

"Why did I just get sworn in as admiral in the middle of the night?" she asked me.

I grinned. "Because Commander Ledger pushed my buttons."

That made her smile. "Aisling, what's going on?"

I handed her the gloves. "Luska sent a letter addressed to me. Wear gloves in case of poison."

She went very still then, raising one eyebrow, but nodded and donned the white gloves. As she read the note, her eyebrows climbed higher and higher. When she finished, she set the letter down, took off the gloves, and began to pace. Elaine was a fearsome warrior in battle, but the greatest thing about her was her mind. Second to my father, she had one of the best minds I knew. She got top marks in psychological warfare. She was a little insane in her revenge plots, much like Tetra, and that's what I needed now.

"Tell me what you're thinking," I finally said after a few minutes.

"You have to reply," she said, and I nodded. I agreed. The bastard asked for my hand in marriage and then threatened my sisters! That could not be met with silence.

She rubbed her hands together and grinned. "Oh, I'm so

tempted to have you respond yes to the marriage proposal and feed him poison in his sleep."

I nodded because I'd considered it, too. "But so much could go wrong. I wouldn't even make it down the aisle likely, and it would involve my signing some type of peace deal."

Which wouldn't be peace. It would be a hostile takeover. They'd strip our mines, rape our women, and turn Amersea into a wasteland. I'd rather die.

"He threatened your sisters," she growled.

I nodded. "I have nothing on him. I didn't even know he existed before today. It seems my father was putting a lot of effort into maximum casualties and not into gathering intel. We need more spies."

Elaine stopped then and met my gaze. "I have an idea."

A thrill went through me because the look on her face was divine. Whatever idea this was, it was going to be good.

"Tell no one else of this letter. Order Commander Ledger to keep it quiet. Give me two days."

I frowned. "Two days for what?"

She spoke in a string of such perfect Luskin, it took me aback. I knew she knew a little Luskin, but that sounded fluent. "What does that mean?"

"It means before I became your governess, I was training to be a spy. I speak fluent Luskin, and I'm going to get something from this Maxim that will scare him straight. We need to mess with his head, let him know you aren't weak, and that if he touches your sisters, you will come for his throat while he sleeps."

I frowned. "Elaine, when I said we needed spies, I didn't mean you!"

"Why not me?" She put a hand on her hip.

Well, for one she was pushing fifty—but I'd never say that. "If he knows about the triplets, he might recognize you."

She waved me off. "No one will recognize me. Not even you."

What? But she looked so determined I didn't want to say no.

"What about taking a team of—?"

"No. I must go alone, or it will be suspicious."

"Elaine, I can count the number of people I care about on one hand," I told her. "If anything happens to you—"

"I trust no one else with this. This young generation is too soft to do what needs to be done," she growled.

Yikes, that sounded like good ol' Elaine.

"Two days?" I asked her.

She nodded once.

"You'll take Vespa?"

"I would never leave her," Elaine confirmed.

Liana was still gone. I wished she was here to counsel me.

I blew out the breath I'd been holding. "Okay. I'll see you in two days."

I prayed I wouldn't regret that.

We both stood there awkwardly, stiffly. I wanted to hug her but wasn't sure if that was too emotional, especially now that I was empress.

Screw it.

I crossed the space and pulled her into my arms. She was stiff for a half second and then sighed, holding me close. "I never had children because I didn't want a weakness people could exploit," she said and pulled back to look at me. "And now I have four."

"You're one of the last weaknesses I have left," I told her. "Don't get caught and let them use you against me."

She gave me a wry grin. "Every good spy travels with a cyanide pill in case of capture."

"Elaine!" I scolded her. She'd better not.

She grinned. "Oh it's good to be back in action. I'll see you in two days," she said and then left the room.

Her age wouldn't stop her. If anything, she looked refreshed at the thought of sneaking into enemy territory and posing as a Luskin spy. And I just let her go? What was I thinking?

I peered at the letter and I knew.

My sisters. This Maxim a-hole had threatened my sisters. Elaine took their safety as seriously as I did. She wouldn't let that go unchecked.

I folded the letter and then there was a knock at the door.

Commander Ledger was there, this time showered and in Fleet-issued fatigues.

"Colt is back..." he said with an air of wonder in his voice.

"That's great! Is he hurt?"

"No, but I think you'd better see this."

I ran to my room, brushed my teeth and changed quickly. Five flights of stairs later, I was topside and staring at the blue griffin that had killed Colt's creature.

Colt was riding it.

"You bonded him?" I staggered forward.

He nodded, grinning. "I'm still upset over the loss of Mara, but... it's hard to explain. I couldn't kill him. The bond started, and now I understand why he did it."

I peered at Commander Ledger, who was watching Colt with interest.

"What are you thinking?" I asked him.

He glanced over at me with a questioning gaze. "Where did you find your Talanagi when you bonded Liana?"

Oh, that... well, might as well let that secret out.

"Luska side of the Wall. I found an old map that showed that's where they are."

"Those bastards!" Ledger slapped his thigh. "I knew it. I knew that's why they had a higher concentration in their ranks."

An idea sprang forth.

"I don't think we should rip the Wall down. That would be a disaster. But what about at the next Lottery... we lead a select few candidates to where we know the Talanagi are?" I said.

To the Luska side of the Wilds is what I didn't say.

The commander and Colt both nodded. "We need to even the playing field long-term," Commander Ledger said.

It was decided. Next Lottery, we'd pick the strongest dozen candidates and show them where to find a Talanagi in the hopes we could add more of them to our ranks.

"Speaking of Talanagi, where is your creature, Empress?" Commander Ledger asked. "Didn't you say she'd be back soon?"

I was starting to seriously worry, but I had way too much going on and I was too tired and hungry to let it affect me.

"She'll show up," I told him, then looked at Colt. "Congratulations on the new bonding. Let's get underground until Luska is done with their retaliation."

CHAPTER NINE

But all day and another night, it was eerily quiet. The base, the Wall, the surrounding area, there had been no attack since we took down their Red Palace and killed the prime leader.

Was it because they were grappling with their loss and burying their dead? Were they swearing in Maxim, and was he waiting until I replied to act? My mind swirled, and all the while, Onyx and Liana were unreachable.

Tonight, Tetra and the rest of our alliance would show up to fulfill their orders, and the base was currently in a lockdown, unsure of what to expect next.

After a full day of more meetings, as I was passing down a long hallway in search of the mess hall for a late dinner, a side door opened, and I yelped until I saw Kohen grinning.

He pulled me into the small room and shut the door, pinning my back against it.

My heart fluttered in my chest. I'd barely seen him. I'd been busy in meetings and learning the ropes of the new base. I was still getting introduced to squad leaders and learning about what my new schedule would be. Student by day, empress by night. That's what we'd decided on. I'd train with Tetra and the rest of my squadron as rookie recruits from sunup to sundown, and then I'd have meetings at night to deal with empress things. On weekends, I was permitted to fly back to Riverine to see my sisters and have more meetings there.

I was already sick of the meetings.

"Tell me you have intel on our creatures. I'm freaking out," I told him.

He smiled. "I don't."

I frowned. "Then why are you smiling?"

He leaned in, sniffing my neck and dragging his lips along my jaw until they rested on mine.

Everything within me disarmed around him. It was like all of the survival techniques I was taught my entire life were blanked from my mind when Kohen was present.

"I had a vision of you," he whispered as he dragged his lips tantalizingly over mine, not stopping until he reached my ear. Heat bloomed through my body so fast and hot, I genuinely wondered if I'd catch fire.

I moaned and reached out to grasp his biceps. This man

would be my ruin. I'd never been more infatuated with another soul than I was with him. But I'd never tell him that.

"And...?" I asked as he kissed my collarbone, tendrils of heat traveling to my core.

Kohen pulled back and just gave me a half-cocked smirk. "I'm not telling. It's for me to know and you to live out."

I punched his shoulder, and he just grinned wider.

"Hey, not fair!" I told him.

He glanced at my lips, grinning like a mad fool, and I couldn't help but match his smile. Kohen was like a drug; his very presence intoxicated me. "Was it a good vision?" I asked.

"The best yet." He licked his lips. I equally loved and hated the anticipation of kissing him. There was something thrilling about knowing he'd had a good vision about me and not knowing it. I'd get to live it out like he said.

"Our love..." He finally kissed my lips before pulling away. "...will rewrite history." He kissed me again, harder, deeper, and I opened myself to him. Was that the vision? That our love would rewrite history, or was he just making a romantic statement?

Did I even care?

I was drowning in this kiss, willingly losing myself to all things Kohen, when I heard a pair of boots clomping down the hall, and we both froze. I pulled back, and Kohen reached up and placed his hand over my frantically beating heart. Then he cocked his head to the side, looking past me and appearing to concentrate deeply. "Onyx just got back. Liana's not with him."

That was all I needed to hear. I sidestepped him and threw the door open. Luckily, no one was in the hallway because I stepped out, smoothing my hair and making sure my shirt was still tucked in.

"Where is she? What happened?" I asked frantically.

Kohen's head was still cocked, brows bunched, as he led the way to the stairwell that would take us outside. We were still living in the underground bunker, expecting Luska to attack.

He was quiet for three flights of stairs and then turned to me. "They killed Drak. But Liana died protecting Onyx."

"She what!" I screeched.

He lowered his voice. "Relax, she's being reborn in the woods. It will just take time before she can get back here."

Relax? My freaking creature died. Even if she was immortal, it was still stressful. "The Luskins could get to her," I whispered back. "Onyx should have stayed with her."

Kohen shook his head. "Liana ordered him to come back and protect you."

I didn't need protection. I needed her to be okay!

I frantically searched our bond, only to feel it shut down like a steel door.

When we reached the top, there was a guard at the door who stood stiffly and saluted me as I passed. When we stepped outside, Kohen took three large steps away from me, so it didn't look like we'd walked out together. Commander Ledger was standing out in the open, watching Onyx with curiosity.

Kohen strode right over to his creature and stroked his neck as Commander Ledger turned to face me. "Where's yours?" he asked.

"Delayed," I responded, gutted that she was all alone in Luska without me.

'Where are you? I'll come get you,' I sent to her but got no response.

Admiral Caruso crossed the quad with a few soldiers at her side and motioned for me to join them.

I saluted the commander and then passed Kohen and Onyx.

"Liana's not responding to me," I whispered to Kohen as I passed.

"She's conserving energy for the rebirth," he told me.

I growled. I didn't like this. Not one bit. The red dragon rider could find her and put another one of those nets over her to keep her from fully being reborn.

But she had survived a thousand years without me—I had to trust she'd be able to survive another few days.

Admiral Caruso saluted me, as did the two men and one woman beside her. I glanced at the rank pins on their uniform to see that they were lieutenants. The female looked particularly badass, with a shaved head and the small amount of hair she did have dyed hot pink. A white snake creature was coiled up her arm.

"These are your instructors," the admiral said. "Combs..." She pointed to the pink-haired female. "Hammer..." She gestured to a male with long dark hair and broody eyes who was missing a finger on his right hand. "And Rahul..." She pointed to a light brown-skinned male with short-cropped hair and brown eyes.

"Imbrian?" I asked Rahul.

"Half," he said, giving no more and no less information.

I nodded. "Will you be instructing the others from Riverine who've been posted here?"

Because Tetra, Alek, Roc, Meera, Dev, Kian, and Anika were due at any moment.

Combs, the female who stood stiffly, flicked her gaze to me. "Yes, Empress."

Two words. They were not a chatty bunch.

"Alright, well, thanks for your service to the Fleet." I saluted them, and they saluted back.

As they left, Admiral Caruso stepped over to me and raised one eyebrow. Her eye was no longer swollen shut, but her face was still covered in bruises. "I haven't seen Lieutenant Steele around..."

It was an open-ended question.

"Mmmm," was all I said.

"She mentioned she might be gone for a few days."

I trusted Caruso, but also I didn't trust anyone.

"She will," I confirmed, and her eyes narrowed.

"Does this have to do with your missing creature?"

Ouch, right for the heart.

"No," I said, though as empress, I didn't need to say anything.

"Then is has to do with the top-secret letter I saw being delivered late last night. Commander Ledger won't say what it was."

This woman was relentless. I sighed, too tired to debate. "Yes, and I will let you and the other admirals in on the contents of the letter when she gets back."

Her interest piqued, she said nothing more. Instead, she looked at the sky. "Why haven't they retaliated for bringing down their Red Palace?"

I knew why. Maxim was waiting on my reply to his ridiculous marriage proposal.

"Any luck on finding my father's killer?" I wanted to change the topic until I was ready to talk to the admirals about the fact that the new Luskin prime leader asked me to wed him.

She nodded. "Found a new lab. Telling no one where it is. Results should take about three to four days."

I blew air through my teeth.

"What if it was one of us?" I asked her.

Her lips pursed into a thin line. "Then I'll spend my life interrogating every single Amersean until I find out who it was and bring you their head."

Her vow was touching. I reached out and squeezed her elbow. "Thank you."

She peered at me and nodded once. "Your father was not a kind man, but he was a damn good leader. He didn't deserve that."

Your father was not a kind man.

Those words unfortunately rang true, and maybe that's why they didn't sting. There was nothing soft or loving about him. But he was a provider, a safety net for my sisters and I growing up in a world without our mother. He did the best he could, and it was good enough. I wasn't going to complain about my lot in life. I'd led a very privileged existence, so not having a father who doted on me wasn't something I was going to cry about at night.

No. It was chin up. Move on.

"Don't worry about your instructors or your friends or Elaine. I've already questioned them, and they are clear. Anyone in close contact with you has been—"

"You questioned Tetra?" I asked her, offense in my voice. "Did you hurt her?"

Now she looked offended. "No. That's not how my power works. Unless they won't talk, then..." She opened her hands as if to say, then she hurt them.

"So they all... talked?"

She nodded. "Sang like canaries. Gave an entire breakdown of the night your father died. Not a single lie."

Relief rushed through me so fast I was breathless. I

hadn't realized how much I'd needed to hear that. Not about Tetra, but the others. It was good to know my inner circle was clean.

"That's good."

She scanned the base and all of the people milling about. "But someone did it. And if they blew the blood lab and are trying to cover it up, I'll find them," she vowed. She saluted me before walking off.

She was right. Someone did do it, likely a person in Amersea. There was no reason to cover up an assassination from Luska. What stories would his blood tell?

Movement at the front gates pulled my attention. My personal driver, Verik's, car pulled through, and I grinned. Tetra was sitting in the front seat with who I assumed were the rest of the alliance in the two rows in back because all of their creatures ran at the sides, flanking the left and right of the car. Or flew, in Alek's and Dev's case. Seeing Dev's creepy vulture caused a chill to race up my spine, more so because I'd heard that if she touched you with one swipe of her talons, you would drop dead.

Meera's little fox running alongside Roc's lynx kept up with the car's speed easily. Anika's lioness was so badass, racing effortlessly next to Tetra's wolf and Kian's monkey creature. They looked like old friends running together, and that made me happy. If creatures liked each other, then it meant their humans did, too. I'd be busy now that I was empress, so Tetra having someone else to look out for her was a good thing.

When the car pulled to a stop, the creatures fanned out, peering around at the space as the doors opened, and one by one, they all stepped out.

They wore their Fleet-issued fatigues and held duffle bags stiffly in their hands as they stood with backs erect and saluted me.

I tried to keep the grin off my face.

"At ease," I said.

They relaxed, looking at me as if wondering if things would change now that I was empress.

"You guys are crazy to want to be posted here," I told them.

Anika hefted her bag and walked over to me. She shrugged. "I hear the food is decent."

I grinned. "It's not bad."

She gripped my shoulder and squeezed before walking past me.

"Hey, old friend," I heard Kohen call to her and glanced over my shoulder just in time to see him open his arms and pull her into a hug. Jealously sliced through my heart like a hot knife, but before I could dwell on it, Tetra was before me.

She was holding hands with Dev. Okay... so that was definitely a thing. He held her duffle as she used her other hand to grip her cane.

"Please tell me Lieutenant Ashendell isn't here," she

begged, dropping Dev's hand and pulling me in for a hug, which I returned.

I laughed. "She's not, but I met our new instructors today, and they seem... uptight."

"Great," Roc said as he came up behind Tetra with Kian at his side. They all walked over to where Kohen and Anika were talking near Onyx.

"Thanks for keeping us all together," Meera said meekly as she reached out and squeezed my hand.

Then, I was standing in front of Alek.

Sweet, handsome, loyal Alek.

He swallowed hard, his eyes running the length of me. "Aisling... I..." He met my gaze, and I was taken aback by the depth there, the emotion and vulnerability. "I'm so sorry to hear about your father."

My father. Not the emperor. He recognized that I'd lost my only parent. My throat clogged with emotion, and I nodded. "Thank you, Alek."

He glanced behind me at everyone talking to Kohen and gave me a weak salute. "I'm going to find my assigned bunk and get settled in. It's been a long journey," he said, picking up his duffle and walking off. Iniki flew down and landed on his shoulder, peering back at me.

Why did I feel sad when I saw Alek? Well, not sad for me. Sad for him. I felt bad at how things had transpired between us. He'd put himself out there, and I'd shot him down.

Would I have said yes to something with Alek if Kohen hadn't existed?

Maybe... but Kohen did exist, and Alek was great... but he wasn't Kohen.

"Come join us." Kohen's deep voice washed over my left shoulder, and my stomach tightened.

I spun, trying to hold off my grin. Stars, he had such a hold over me. Looking at him now, I couldn't stop thinking about our kiss in the small closet room. I'd never been more attracted to a man.

"Join you where?" I asked, raising one eyebrow.

"There is a bar of sorts on base," Kohen said and then walked over to the others.

I followed him. I'm pretty sure if my father were alive, he'd council me not to go with my friends to the bar on base as acting empress.

CHAPTER TEN

The "bar" was a glorified mess hall that became the hangout spot from 8 p.m. onwards. Fleet personnel of all ages and ranks fanned out across tables and let their hair down. Some music was playing out of a speaker in the corner, and some people were drinking alcohol while others, probably on duty, sipped water.

They stiffened as I passed, sitting up straighter and standing at attention. Elaine would probably advise against fraternizing with the common soldiers. My father never did. But I wasn't my father, and I wanted to be different.

"At ease," I said as I walked by them. One by one, they all went back to muffled talking or dancing, but they still glanced nervously my way as if wondering why I was there. I noticed they weren't just looking at me. They were glancing at Kohen and the other Imbrians with me in a suspicious manner. I hated it. I hated the division between us, but it had been there for so long that I wasn't sure how to bridge the gap. As empress, I should be able to do something about that. Maybe it started small, maybe it started with me sitting at a table with my friends who were Imbrian and having a good time. Let the soldiers see us smiling and laughing the night away.

I realized then that there was a newfound freedom now that my father was gone. I felt guilty for thinking it, but now that I knew his disapproval wasn't imminent, I could do what I wanted to a certain degree.

"It will take getting used to," Tetra whispered to me as she braced herself on her cane. "An empress of the people," she declared.

I grinned at my bestie, glad to have her with me.

We found a spot in the corner, and the second we sat down, Anika reached out and clasped my shoulder, keeping her voice low. "You blew their Red Palace sky high. That deserves a toast."

Everyone chorused their agreement, and Meera disappeared with Dev to grab drinks and dinner.

"Hey, it wasn't just me." I tipped my head to Kohen, and Anika pulled her hand from my shoulder with a nod.

Was there jealousy on her face?

The drinks were served, water and juice for all of us, because we had to report for duty early in the morning. Nachos with candied shredded pork were set before me by

Tetra. I said nothing when Kohen took a sip of my drink and a bite of my food first and then pushed it back in front of me after a few moments. He'd somehow become my food tester when Elaine wasn't around. I'd protested yesterday, saying I didn't want anything to happen to him, but he'd argued that we were both alive well into the future, so he wasn't worried about it.

Anika raised her glass. "To *everyone* involved in bringing justice to the Luskins."

The table roared their approval, but they had no idea. No one had any idea that we'd killed Prime Leader Vlek when we'd attacked that building. Word had spread about the building going down, and it had boosted morale, but once I shared the contents of that letter with the admirals, the assassination of Luska's highest commanding officer, who had tortured our people for decades, would spread like wildfire. If they were excited now, they'd be thrilled when they heard that. But I trusted Elaine in this matter and wanted to execute her plan first and foremost before I told any of the admirals.

"Room for a few more?" Jace's voice came from behind me, and I stiffened.

I turned, seeing his best friend, Tucker, beside him, both holding their duffle bags.

Of course they would be here. His own father was. After what he'd said about me not "putting out," I didn't want him here, but I didn't want to act petty.

Tetra stood at the same time as Kohen.

"Table's full," she growled. There were easily four more spots. It was a huge mess hall table.

Oh, thank the stars for sassy best friends who do your dirty work for you.

Jace rolled his eyes. "Oh come on, Tetra. We're going to be working and training together. At some point we need to move past this."

"The table is *full*." Kohen echoed Tetra's words, but there was a warning in his tone.

Jace glanced at me, pleading in his gaze. How had I ever loved him? He was such a vapid jerk.

"Get lost, Jace. Make new friends," I spat.

His head reeled back like he'd been slapped. Maybe that's what he needed—for me to finally lay down the law. He'd said Kohen shouldn't waste time on me because I didn't put out, and he'd cheated on me. In what world did he think I would ever tolerate his presence more than I had to?

"And you're still here. Wow, this is pathetic," Anika said.

Tucker pulled Jace's arm, and he snapped out of his shock, anger marring his features. They turned and walked away.

An awkward silence descended on the table.

"Remember that time those thugs on the south hill kept messing with us?" Meera asked.

Dev, Kian, Kohen, and Anika all looked at Meera then,

who wore a maniacal grin. "I have the herbs for it in my pack."

"For what?" I asked.

Kohen peered at me. "If we tell you, then you're complicit in the act."

I raised one eyebrow. "What act?"

He shrugged. "Just a little something to humble, Jace."

Tetra was smiling too, now. "Oh, I like this. Tell me."

Kohen peered at me one last time as if giving me a chance to leave so I wouldn't overhear.

"I'm empress. I'm pretty sure I can get away with murder, though I hope you're not planning that. He *is* the commander's son."

Meera leaned in. "*Gratonis bulgaris* root. Even in small quantities, it has *quite* the laxative effect."

We all burst out laughing, drawing the gazes of some near us. I hadn't expected that. It was so innocent, and yet perfect for Jace.

"Oh yes please," I agreed with their plan.

Meera simply nodded. "Consider it done by breakfast."

I peered around the table at our little alliance and smiled. Never in a million years did I think I'd become close, trusting friends of nearly half a dozen Imbrians. There was just one person missing: Alek. I glanced at Roc, and he gave me a small smile as if reading my mind.

Was he really tired or had he said that because things were weird between us?

"Speaking of herbs..." Anika lowered her voice and glanced at me. "Any way we could get leave for a few days to head back to Imbria and get... the stuff I need?"

Right. I'd almost forgotten the convulsions and the small herbal chews she took to stave it off.

"Of course," I told her. "Can you wait until the weekend? I'll say you're visiting family."

She nodded.

I looked at Meera. "Can you get enough to last a long time?"

Meera, so small and delicate and clearly brilliant, nodded her head. "I'll make a year's worth in this batch."

Good. I wanted to avoid Anika having any more episodes.

I tucked into my nachos and listened to a hilarious story Tetra was telling about how she'd tricked Valor into thinking blue corn was poison when she was small. Then I felt Liana stir in my mind.

I stiffened.

'I'm reborn. Coming home,' Liana sent, and I sagged with relief. Kohen met my gaze and smiled. Onyx must have told him.

'I was worried sick about you!' I told her. *'Did you get revenge for your mate?'*

Even though Onyx already said they had, I wanted to hear it from her.

'Yes.' I could hear the grin in her voice. But there was something else. Something she was hiding.

'What aren't you telling me?' I asked.

"So I was thinking, tomorrow after training—" Anika began, and I stood, fake yawning.

"Sorry, I'm beat. I'm gonna head out," I told everyone.

They wished me goodbye, and I knew Kohen wanted to talk with me more about Liana, but he didn't. It would look like we were a couple. I'd convinced Elaine and Caruso to let me ditch a security detail while on base. I was a weapon myself, being able to explode into fire, and they agreed.

'I saw some things while I was here. Things that have me worried about the future of Amersea at the hands of this new leader,' Liana said.

I sucked in a breath, making it to the door and then out of the mess hall. *'Maxim?'*

'Yes. He's... Aisling. He...' She was struggling to put it into words.

'What is it?' I was fully freaked out now. If it worried her, it should definitely worry me.

'He has two bondeds. Two creatures.'

I stopped walking and cocked my head to the side. What did she just say? *'That's not possible,'* I said, but as I did, I wondered... maybe it was. Had anyone ever tried?

'That's not the worst part, Aisling. He's... evil.'

Evil?

'What do you mean?' Liana and I had different cultures and upbringings. Evil to her might be something different to me.

I felt her struggle to explain. *'Your father, his energy was... off-putting to me. I never liked him...'* The confession didn't shock me, which made me feel weird. Had I always known she didn't like him? Yes, I think I did. Deep down.

She'd once told me she was an amazing judge of character, and for her not to like my father should be offensive, but I guess I understood. He was prickly and often unkind.

'Maxim is nothing like that, Aisling. His energy... when I look at him, bile rises in my throat. He's... I'm trying to think of the word in my language and translate it. He's the lack of light.'

Lack of light. Darkness? That caused chills to race up my arms.

'He asked me to marry him,' I blurted out.

I felt her fiery rage. *'Not while I'm still alive! And I'm immortal, so that's saying a lot.'*

I smiled at that and then quickly told her about the letter Maxim sent and Elaine and her mission.

'Elaine is here, in Luska? I will find her and fly her home.'

'No, it's danger—' Then I remembered that she was immortal. *'Okay, but how will you find her?'*

'If I have smelled someone once, I can find them almost anywhere.'

Wow. That was a good skill to have.

'Okay, well, stay out of sight. She's gone incognito, spying,' I told her.

'I'll keep to the woods. There are plenty of those here.'

Nervousness ate away at my gut as I stepped back down

into the bunker and made my way to my room. How much longer would we all stay down here before there was no retaliation attack? Is that what Maxim was waiting for? For us to go topside and relax, and then he'd bomb the base? What Liana said about him having no light and being evil, gave me chills.

I paced my room, checking in with Liana every hour.

'I found her. I almost didn't recognize her,' Liana said.

I sagged in relief. *'Is she alive?'*

I could nearly feel Liana's grin. *'She's more than alive, Aisling. She got something that will scare the life out of that demon.'*

Demon? Wow, Liana really didn't like Maxim.

'What did she get?'

'I'll let her show you. Be back in about four hours. Get some sleep.'

Sleep! No way. I'd pace this entire bedroom until they got back and would only sleep when Elaine was safe in her bed, and I knew what she got that would scare Maxim. I needed to reply to his letter and to tell the admirals about it. I also had my first day of base training tomorrow morning.

No. I'd sleep when I was dead.

CHAPTER ELEVEN

'W*e're here.*' Liana spoke into my mind, and I leaped up from the table. I'd been sipping coffee in my room and browsing a book in an effort to stay awake. I took the stairs two at a time. It was just about 2 a.m. but the base was still crawling with Fleet soldiers. They saluted as I passed, backs ramrod straight against the wall.

I burst out of the door the second I hit the top floor, passing the two guards there and skidding to a stop before Liana and...

Who the hell was that?

A beautiful woman with long blonde hair wearing fishnet stockings, a red corset, and black leather shorts got off of Liana. As the woman approached me, I stared at her ample cleavage, then my gaze went to her face. She wore heavy makeup, red lipstick, and—

"Elaine!" I hissed, staggering backward.

My eyes! I wanted to look away from my governess, but she grinned, ripping the blonde wig off of her head and saluting me.

"You. Have. Boobs," I said stupidly.

She laughed.

I'd lived with the woman my entire life, and she'd always been so covered up. Button-up shirts, turtlenecks, hair in a bun, no makeup. This was... traumatizing.

"And I used them to infiltrate Maxim's very innermost bedroom chambers," she countered.

My eyes widened. "You what? Did you... with him?"

She grimaced. "No way. I put the charm on his guard, though, and then killed him."

That sounded more like Elaine.

I peered at Liana, standing behind her, and I wanted to run to her and check on her, but my curiosity held me in place. Vespa, who I hadn't noticed before, leaped from his seat in the saddle and came up beside Elaine.

"Liana said you got something that will scare Maxim?"

She nodded, "We are ready to write him back now, Empress, and with your letter you can include these."

She pulled some black cloth from her bag and opened it tautly for me to inspect.

They were black silk boxers with the word *Maxim* embroidered into the waistband in gold thread.

"Ewww, are these his underwear?" I asked her. But I was grinning.

She nodded, unable to hide her own smile. "And when you send them back with a letter telling him to 'Sleep tight,' he'll think we have a spy in his midst. Or at least a way to get to him if he messes with us. He'll tear his innermost circle apart, searching for the traitor."

Whoa. Okay, that was genius.

I yawned, and she patted my shoulder. "I'll bring these to your living quarters, and we can work on the letter in the morning."

I nodded. "I have to tell the admirals."

Elaine shrugged. "You don't have to do anything, but I agree you should. Let's tell them after we've sent the letter so we don't have to get their opinion on anything."

Hah. I liked that.

"Deal."

She left to go inside and hopefully change clothes because seeing her like this was like seeing your own mother indecent.

I finally walked over to Liana and hugged her neck, stroking her feathers. "I'm glad you both got home safely," I told her.

I could sense that she felt some healing and closure at

finally killing Drak for her mate, but there was something bothering her.

She peered down at me. *'Aisling, don't underestimate Maxim.'*

I felt something inside of her, something I hadn't ever felt from her before.

Fear.

'It will be okay,' I told her, and then wished her goodnight.

But that night, I tossed and turned.

Demon.

Absence of light.

Liana's warning circled around my head all night long.

Early in the morning, after only a few hours' sleep, Elaine shook me awake while holding a giant cup of coffee.

"We need to respond to his letter," she told me.

I marched myself out of bed and shuffled over to the bathroom, where I got ready quickly and then chugged the coffee.

We sat down at the table and reread Maxim's letter together quickly.

Empress Aisling,

Tonight, your attack on our Red Palace killed my father, Prime Leader Vlek.

I've waited two decades to take over the war efforts from my weak father. So, I wanted to say thank you for giving me this opportunity. I'm going to give you two options now, and I'd like you to choose very carefully.

1. Marry me, unite our people, and surrender your country, lands, and ember to me, and I will not harm anything you hold dear, including your three beautiful sisters.

2. Deny my hand, and I'll strip your lands of their people, mine all of your ember, and kill each and every one of your sisters before forcing you to be my wife.

I await your reply,
Maxim

SMOKE CURLED out of my nostrils and Elaine placed a calming hand over mine.

"You must be equally bold," she warned.

I nodded, and then I wrote.

Maxim darling,

You are so welcome for helping rid the world of your pig-headed father. I cannot wait to also take your life and end the war, absorbing your people and lands into my own and finally giving them a proper leader.

My answer to your question is this...

If you ever threaten me or my sisters again, I'll remove you of your manhood. Please accept the enclosed gift as proof that I can do that.

Sleep tight. I'll be watching.

Empress Aisling

"It's perfect," Elaine said, folding the boxers on top and then placing them in a package before sealing. I was livid, pacing the floor and thinking about the audacity of this man.

"Liana said he has two creatures and that he's evil," I told Elaine.

She paused in my doorway, turning around to face me with a shadow of fear over her face. "I never saw him in my time there, but I did see the red rider you speak of. She's his twin sister."

Oh crap.

I sagged onto the bed, my heart racing in my chest. Red

rider was Maxim's twin! She was the prime leader's daughter? Now it made sense why she said I killed her father that night. She knew my secret... She...

"Elaine, get inside and shut the door," I said before my governess could leave and deliver the letter. I knew it was a risk, but I could trust Elaine. She'd proven that.

"I have to tell you something." I couldn't meet her gaze.

Liana sensed what I was about to do and her presence rose up in me. *'You tell her, but no one else. Ever. Not your sisters or Tetra or anyone.'*

If Elaine was going to be advising me, she had to know everything.

Elaine was very still, watching me like a mother watches a daughter who is about to confess something.

She waited, peering over at me with curiosity.

"I have a power I haven't told you about. A secret power."

She peered over her shoulder to make sure the door was indeed closed and then walked over to me until she was standing right before me.

"Who knows about this power?" she asked.

I swallowed hard. "Kohen, Liana, and... the red rider, Maxim's twin sister."

Did anyone else know? Maybe all of Luska for all I knew.

Elaine's eyebrows rose when I mentioned the red rider knowing what my power was. "Is it what I overheard in your father's office the night he died?" Then she lowered her voice. "The power to see the future?"

Crap. I'd forgotten about that. I'd burst into my father's office and told him I had Kohen's power so I could save the training center from the attack.

I shook my head. "That... was a lie," was all I said because I didn't want her to know about Kohen.

Now her brows knitted together in the middle of her forehead.

"Would telling me the truth put you in danger?"

I loved that she was always worried about my safety. It was proof I could trust her.

"Only if you told someone," I said.

"I'd never tell a soul a secret you shared with me in confidence, Aisling." Her voice was soft and filled with compassion.

I took a shaky breath and exposed my truth: "I can enthrall people. Control their minds."

Her face fell as she stared at me in wonder, and then a fierceness came over her. "The red rider knows this?" she growled.

I nodded. "I had to use my power to help in the attack on Riverine."

She chewed her lip. "Then Maxim knows. *That's* why he wants you as his wife. He wants to use you to control others."

My stomach bottomed out. She was probably right. "Well, he couldn't. I'd control him before he ever got within ten feet of me."

She appeared lost in thought. "Maybe... yeah, I hope so."

She sounded unsure. The way she and Liana feared him made *me* fear him.

"Should we still send the letter?" I asked.

She nodded. "Absolutely. Nothing changes." She walked to the door and turned to look over her shoulder. "And Aisling?"

"Yes?" I looked up at her.

"We never speak of this power again. It's safer that way."

I nodded, swallowing hard.

She let out a shaky breath and grasped the handle of the door to my living quarters, yanking it open and then shutting it behind her.

Now to call a meeting with the commander and the admirals...

CHAPTER TWELVE

"Marry you!" Admiral Caruso screamed as she stared at the letter that sat open-faced on the war table. The other admirals present, the five I could muster on short notice, huffed their disapproval.

"Who cares about that nonsense? She killed Prime Leader Vlek! *That's* what we focus on," Admiral Blade said.

Nods of agreement made their way around the table.

"I say we distribute an official letter from the empress to the people of Amersea stating that she has killed the prime leader of Luska in retaliation for her father," Commander Ledger said. "It will make her look strong."

More nods of agreement. Then they looked at me.

"I'm fine with that, but it wasn't just me. I had help," I told them.

They waved me off.

"You lead this Fleet. Their win is your win," Caruso said. "Now, what should we respond to this Maxim character who proposed marriage and then threatened to kill your sisters?"

Elaine and I shared a wry grin.

"Oh, I've already responded," I told them.

Every single person in the room froze as if made of ice. Their heads slowly pivoted to me. Admiral Blade's tone was accusatory. "What? When? How long have you had this letter?"

"You have no right to question the empress in such a way!" Elaine snapped, and the admiral's cheeks pinked.

I pulled out a copy of the letter Elaine and I had sent. She'd made one so that we could show them. I laid it on the table.

As they read, I watched as each and every one smiled at my response, and then Commander Ledger peered up at me. "What gift did you give him?"

Elaine and I had talked about this. I was well within my right to send people out on covert operations and not tell them.

"A pair of his underwear that I had stolen from his very room," I answered.

Ledger's mouth opened, and he glanced at Elaine, who just raised one eyebrow.

"We're sending spies into Luska now? Your father never did that," Admiral Blade said.

"When we need to, yeah, we are. And maybe my father should have," I responded. Silence covered the room.

"I think we're done here." Elaine popped up and walked over to the table. "Due to the response in our letter, which I just delivered to a messenger at the Wall an hour ago, I suggest we evacuate the entire base back down into the bunker for the next forty-eight hours and put our perimeter troops on high alert."

Commander Ledger didn't seem to like her calling the shots, but he nodded. "I agree."

Fifteen minutes later, I was in the bunker in a gymnasium training room with the alliance, Kohen, and our instructors.

"Holy stars, Aisling, is it true you killed Prime Leader Vlek when you collapsed that building?" Anika asked.

"What?" Everyone chimed in and moved closer to listen.

I shared a look with Kohen, and he nodded. The word was officially out. I'd told Kohen during one of our closet rendezvous.

Kohen knew Vlek was gone, but he didn't know about Maxim asking to marry me. Or at least I hadn't told him. Whether or not he had foresight about it, I wasn't sure.

"Yes," I stated, and the room erupted into whoops and cheers, including our instructors.

"So that's why we're living underground," Tetra said.

"Is it true Jace is missing training because he has explosive diarrhea?" I asked Anika, and she grinned as everyone else burst out laughing.

Meera winked. "It happens sometimes."

Before I could say more, the walls shook slightly as a low rumble sounded above us, and everyone's eyes went wide.

'Liana?' I searched for her energy, panicked.

'I'm fine. Out hunting with Onyx.'

A siren blared from somewhere a few floors up, and the instructors walked over to us. "Practice is suspended until further notice. Empress, you are probably needed in the command center."

Right. Because I was a student but also the leader of this nation. My friends gave me some fearful looks as I followed our instructors out the door, where Commander Ledger was waiting in the hallway.

"It was a direct hit. I'm still waiting on a damage report, Empress," he told me as I joined him in making quick strides to the command center on this floor.

"Maxim got my letter," I stated.

The commander nodded. "Yes, he did."

Soldiers barreled past us, yelling orders through the halls.

"I'd rather him angry than quiet," the commander said. "I like predictable people."

It was a fair point. Maxim doing nothing in retaliation

since I'd killed his father was unnerving. *This* was familiar territory.

We entered the command room. Elaine was there wearing a fresh uniform with her new admiral pin. Caruso was there as well. Commander Ledger and I made four.

"I've tripled the guard staff around your sisters back in Riverine," Elaine said as I walked in, and I nodded, feeling relieved. If Maxim did try to honor his word, then my sisters might be in danger. Though, I slept better knowing they were in the little, unassuming house with the giant willow tree.

I didn't really know what we were supposed to do. Talk about the damage? Retaliate immediately? War meetings were the final step in my father's training with me, and I hadn't had many of them.

"I say we send a message back so that this new leader knows we aren't going to tolerate the things his father did the last few decades. A change in power is a good chance to gain a new front in the war," Admiral Caruso said.

Commander Ledger nodded. "What do you suggest?"

Caruso pulled out a map of Luska and pointed to a new inked-in area. "They have a new military base close to the Wall, probably where they are launching from right now. I say we hit them there. Hard."

Ledger raised one eyebrow. "And how did you get this intel on their new base? This is the first I've heard of it."

Caruso glanced at Elaine. "Confirmed sighting by one of our own."

Elaine must have seen it when she was spying on Maxim. Good, she reported it to Caruso.

"Colt has a flying Talanagi creature now. We could drop another payload on it," the commander said.

I shook my head. "They'll be watching the skies like crazy, expecting that after what we did to the Red Palace."

"She's right. We should either launch it over the Wall or send in an elite ground team to rig it to blow," Elaine said.

As they went back and forth over which way was the best way to blow up their new military site, I found myself wondering if this was all war was. Back and forth, back and forth. They bomb us, we bomb them. A hundred years later we can barely remember who started it. I'd grown up in war; it was all I knew. My father had a very strict opinion on peace treaties.

'They're for the weak. And they don't last forever. The only thing that lasts forever is if you control everything.'

In my father's mind, if a country attacked us, he wasn't happy until he was ruling over that country. And I understood that. I did. But I also wondered what the world would be like without war. What it might be like to rule over a country in a time of peace.

"What do you think, Empress?" Commander Ledger asked me.

"Let's launch a counterassault from here. Our men on the

Wall can shoot down any interference to hopefully get it to its target. If that fails, we send in a ground team."

He nodded. "I agree."

Caruso and Elaine agreed as well.

"I recommend you stay down here for the next forty-eight hours. No going topside," the commander said to me.

'Onyx and I will stay nearby, but out of harm's way.' Liana read my mind as I was about to ask him about our creatures. The smaller creatures were down here with their bondeds, but the larger ones had to stay topside.

"Two more days down here?" I questioned.

"Get used to it," the commander snapped and then left to go give the order.

Elaine and Caruso left next, Elaine squeezing my shoulder as she passed, and then I made my way to my room.

Two days of hiding out down here with no more lessons. That sounded incredibly boring.

That night, I lay awake around midnight, having trouble falling asleep. There had been another explosion, not as big as the one before, but enough to knock the chess pieces over on the board in the corner.

A small tap came at my door and I grabbed my dagger, padding over to it.

"Who is it?" I asked, refusing to open it until Elaine or whoever it was announced themselves.

"Your soulmate," Kohen said from the other side, and I grinned, pulling the door open.

"You're so cheesy," I told him.

"You love it," he winked, slipping inside after looking up and down the hallway. I shut the door quickly behind him.

"You can't be seen in here!" I hissed but secretly relished the fact that he was here.

He nodded. "I know. That's why I have been casing out the hallway for the past forty-five minutes."

My heart ratcheted up a notch. Being stuck with Kohen in a broom closet was one thing, but my bedroom was another. If someone saw, they could say we'd slept together. It would be the end of my reputation as—

"Oh, do you play chess?" Kohen walked over to the board and sat down.

Get out of your head, Aisling, I scolded myself.

Walking over to the chessboard, I sat before it. "I've been playing since I was three. My tutor was the grandmaster of Riverine." I moved the black pawn forward one space, and Kohen grinned.

He moved his white pawn forward opposite mine. "I may not have had fancy tutors, but I've also been playing chess since I was small. My father taught me, and then after he... passed, we all played in the orphanage."

Passed was a nicer term than *murdered*. My father *murdered* his. It was the unspoken thing between us.

"About the orphanage," I said, changing the subject. "I

thought we paid for you and your brothers to be properly schooled and raised and stuff." I wasn't really sure what kind of childhood he had. The Blackout started a war with Imbria that took us five years to win, ending with my father killing his. Kohen would have been about ten at the time.

I moved my rook next, and he snort-laughed, quickly pulling out his knight and taking my pawn. Dammit, I was distracted.

"My little brothers and I were thrown into an orphanage in the slums. We went to a government school with all the other poor kids. I was given no special treatment."

I continued to play chess, but my heart wasn't in it. I was thinking about him growing up without parents because of my father.

Kohen shrugged at my silence. "Turns out I didn't need special treatment."

I shifted uncomfortably. He wasn't saying anything mean, but I still felt bad. It was my father's fault he didn't have the childhood he would have had his father still been alive.

"I… I'm sorry for judging you and your friends when I first met you. I was taught wrong," I admitted, unable to meet his gaze. My father told me that Imbrians couldn't be trusted. That they all hated us and would turn on us at any moment. He was wrong.

Kohen's hand slipped across the table and found mine as I moved to pick up a bishop. "I know. It's okay."

I finally looked up into his eyes, and all I found was compassion. I didn't deserve him. I found myself thinking about his gift and all of the visions he'd had about us. I prayed they were true. Every single one.

"If you could give your power back, would you?" I asked.

He froze, contemplating that. "Yes."

I cocked my head to the side in surprise. "The other day you said you liked having your power. That it allowed you to relive the good moments."

He nodded, his face appearing void of emotion. "But it also allows me to see the bad, Aisling."

I frowned. What other bad was there? We'd had the attack on the training campus, my father died, Nikhil died...

"Is there more bad coming?" I asked him.

He looked up at me, sad, and nodded. "You have no idea."

I stopped playing the game, instead hugging my arms to my chest. "Tell me."

He stepped away from the table, getting off his chair to kneel before me. He grasped both sides of my face. "We don't have much time left together. I want our last days to be nice."

Shock ripped through me. "Last days," I croaked. Why didn't we have much time together? What was happening?

He seemed to catch on to what I was thinking and shook his head. "Neither of us dies. But... oh, there are so many things I wish I could tell you. So many things I wish you would just trust me about and take my word for."

I frowned. "Like what? I do trust you." I did. As much as I fought that before, I did trust Kohen. He'd earned it.

He chewed on his lip. "Like about your father."

It felt like ice water had been poured into my veins. "What about my father?!" I snapped.

Kohen sighed, watching me as if I were a coiled snake. Leaning forward, he captured my mouth in a kiss, disarming me immediately. My entire body warmed to his touch, and I parted my lips, letting his tongue spread across mine. I moaned, biting on his bottom lip, and he pulled away panting.

"Same time tomorrow night?" he asked. "We can finish the game." He motioned to the chess match he was winning.

How could I say no to him? To that kiss?

I wanted to know what he was talking about with my father and what bad was coming. But I also didn't. I just wanted to freeze time and keep him and me just like this.

I nodded and got up to follow him out. Opening the door, I scouted the hall, telling him it was safe. Then he ran out like he was never here.

CHAPTER THIRTEEN

"You brat!" Anika playfully growled at Tetra, who had just thrown some chalk powder at her. I slipped into the gym where they were working out, and they both greeted me.

"She cheats," Anika exclaimed, but she was smiling.

Tetra rolled her eyes. "It's called playing every advantage you have."

I liked seeing them close like this, especially for Tetra's benefit, but I'd be lying if I didn't admit I was a little jealous. I hadn't spent much time with my bestie since my father died.

"I had time between meetings. Thought I would say hi." Our training was still paused as the bombs rocked the base outside, and I was in near constant strategy meetings.

"I've got mess hall duty." Anika spit out her tongue. "I'll see you guys later?"

Tetra nodded, and so did I. Anika grabbed her gym bag and left.

It was just Tetra and I in the small workout room. My bestie hobbled over to sit next to me on the bench press.

"Hey, friend." She gave me a small smile, and I knew that she knew I needed to talk.

"Hey," I offered.

"It's been a crazy week," she said.

I nodded, swallowing hard. I was having trouble processing everything that had happened in the last week. It was too much, and I knew this would be my life now, a constant barrage of trauma to process.

"How are you and Dev?" I needed some good news, and when her face broke into a sheepish grin, I knew I'd get it.

"Girl, I like him so much," she confessed, and I laughed.

"Is he nice?" I didn't know Dev that well, but I hoped he wasn't a player.

"The sweetest. Last night I went to my bunk, and there were wildflowers and a note on my pillow."

"Aww." I leaned in and shoulder-bumped my bestie. She had a hard time trusting guys. I loved this for her. He couldn't have gotten wildflowers down here, so that meant he'd snuck out topside to retrieve them for her.

"How's Kohen?" She waggled her eyebrows, and I flicked my gaze to the door to make sure we were alone.

"The sweetest," I winked, using her words. I hadn't said anything about Kohen and my secret little thing we had going on, but after hearing about our kiss on graduation night, I'm sure she knew. She was my best friend. She had to know.

"Aisling, the way he looks at you, it's like you're the biggest piece of ember in the world."

I laughed. "That's an interesting comparison."

"Shut up." She lightly punched me, smiling. "It means you're valuable to him."

We were quiet a moment, and then her hand slipped into mine. "How are you doing with the empress stuff and your dad being gone?"

I heaved a big sigh. "It's a lot."

She nodded, squeezing my hand. "It's going to be okay. You're doing a great job," she told me.

This was what I came for, a Tetra pep talk. I left feeling a little lighter than when I came.

THAT NIGHT, I eagerly awaited for Kohen to come to my room around midnight. When he did, I pulled him inside and we were both grinning ear to ear.

This was love, love in the middle of a war, and I was so excited to see him, to touch him, to kiss him. He never pressured me like Jace had, even though sometimes I wanted him to. Sometimes, I didn't care what would happen if I slept with Kohen. I wanted him, all of him.

We were playing our chess game again, this time with me winning, when I peered over at him.

"What did you mean when you said you want me to trust you about certain things like about my father?" I hedged.

Kohen stiffened. "Aisling, I don't want to do this. Not tonight. It's been such a good night."

It had. We'd told funny stories and kissed until my lips were swollen, and eaten chocolate and played chess. It was almost like a date.

"Why not tonight?" I asked. "And why are you saying more bad is coming? Kohen, I can't relax knowing we might be separated."

He set his chess piece down and looked up at me.

"Please," I begged. "My mind is running wild with scenarios. Will I be kidnapped? Will Tetra die? Just tell me."

He fisted his hand and lightly rapped the side of his head. "I wish I could bash all of the visions out of my skull."

"Don't say that." I reached for him, letting him pull me onto his lap.

"Just tell me," I begged again.

He peered up at me with those impossibly blue eyes. "Remember that day I said it was the last time I'd kiss you in a long time?"

I nodded. He'd said he'd gotten the timing wrong.

Leaning forward, he planted a chaste kiss on my lips. "It's tonight. Tonight is the last night I kiss you for a while."

My stomach dropped, and I suddenly felt sick. "Why?"

He breathed out harshly. "I can't say. You won't believe me... it leads to a fight."

I frowned. "What? Why wouldn't I believe you?"

He'd seen us fight?

He shook his head. "It's too hard to explain, Aisling. Can we just enjoy this time together?" He traced his finger along my collarbone and sent chills down my spine.

"Are we still getting married? In your visions, will I still be your wife?" I asked, trying to understand how we could be separated for a while and fight, but still get married one day. I wasn't sure I fully believed that, but I wanted to. It didn't make sense.

The most beautiful smile graced his face then. "Yes, Aisling. I've seen you as my wife in three different visions now. But it's... a long way off. We take the bumpy road to get there."

I had to admit, I'd come to daydream about some of the things he told me. I couldn't fathom a world where I would be his wife, but I'd come to crave that future. If I were destined to be his wife, why was tonight the last time he would kiss me? Maybe Elaine would find out and ban me from seeing him? Would I? *Probably for a while, yeah.* I had to be sensible. I was the empress.

"One last thing," I asked him, letting him trace over my

skin, causing heat to travel with his finger. "What did you mean about my father and you wish I would believe you? At least tell me that?"

He bristled, stopping his rhythmic motions over my skin. "I shouldn't have said that."

"But you did."

He nodded. "Aisling... your father wasn't a good man. He was hiding things, dark things."

I frowned, my heart beating in my chest like a drum. "What? No. He wasn't perfect, but—"

"No, Aisling, he wasn't even decent," he snapped, and I stepped off of him.

"I understand you harbor ill thoughts of my father because of what he did to yours..."

"It's not that." Kohen stood and stalked forward. "I don't care about that anymore. I care about *you*."

I frowned, confused. I backed off. "I shouldn't have brought this up if this is indeed our last night together—for whatever reason." I folded my arms. He was staring at the wall.

"What are you thinking? Talk to me," I said. I felt desperate to hold on to the last two days. The secret kisses in the closet, him slipping into my room at night; I wanted a million more days like this.

He peered over at me with fire in his gaze. "I'm thinking of how deeply I love you and wondering if I've shown you that enough." He walked over to me. "I'm praying to every star in the sky that you know that every cell in my body aches for you. All the time we'll spend apart, I will be thinking of nothing but you."' He cupped my face in his hands: "Aisling, if you remember anything of me, please remember that everything I do is to protect you."

An overwhelming fear washed over me, my stomach turning to rock and my heart ceasing to beat for a second.

"What did you do, Kohen?"

He leaned forward, pressing his lips to mine in a way that made my soul ache. "It's not just what I've done, it's also what I'm willing to do. I'll burn this entire world down before I let a hair on your head be harmed."

The fear inside of me grew.

"How long will we be apart?" I realized at that moment he was saying goodbye. That's what this was.

A deep sorrow entered his features. "Long enough to slowly kill me inside."

What? I didn't understand? It was starting to scare me.

"Kohen—"

A knock came at my door, and my eyes flew wide. Kohen brushed one more chaste kiss to my lips and then ran to hide behind the door just as I walked over and opened it a crack. It was late, and Elaine was standing there fully in her military fatigues, holding a note. "We got a response," she said.

From Maxim?

"Let's go to the command center, call in Caruso and Ledger. We might need all heads on this one," I told her, praying she wouldn't suggest coming inside my room to read it together.

Her gaze flicked into my room, and I held my breath. Did she know? Could she smell him? Could Vespa, who stood at her side, peering up at me with interest?

"Yes, Empress," she said, revealing nothing, but I could hear the disappointment in her voice.

She knew. She knew Kohen was here, but I was empress now, and there was nothing she could do about it. I stepped out of the room, shutting the door behind me as we walked down the long hallway to the command room.

The guard that stood outside of it saluted us as we approached. "Please go wake Commander Ledger and Admiral Caruso," Elaine said.

He nodded and left his post as I placed my hand on the door to go inside.

Elaine grasped my shoulder, gently stopping me. I looked up at her.

She peered back down the hall in the direction of my room. "I *strongly* advise against that," she said.

I sucked in a breath, waiting for more. Waiting for, *What the hell were you thinking, Aisling? He's Imbrian, and not just any Imbrian, your family's sworn enemy...*

But that was all she said.

"Noted," I responded and stepped into the room.

Maybe that was it. She warned me, and Kohen and I would take a break now so others wouldn't catch us. Yes, that must be what he was walking about. Because I couldn't focus on the alternative. My father was right. Love made you weak. I couldn't let Kohen be my weakness, taking up my thoughts during important meetings. I'd have to trust that everything would be okay.

Elaine laid the thick white envelope on the table as we waited for the others. It was a bulging package with something more than paper in it, which made me nervous for some reason.

The second Caruso and commander Ledger walked in, Elaine updated us all.

"This was given to our messenger on the Wall less than an hour ago. I assume it's from Maxim."

She handed me the bulging envelope, and I tore it open, forgetting about possible poison and wearing gloves. I half expected him to have sent his underwear back to me with some weird marriage proposal to explain the bulky package. But when my eyes landed on the three identical purple bows, I screamed.

Elaine gave a garbled cry as well, and Commander Ledger and Admiral Caruso were asking what it was.

I didn't answer or read the letter. That would be a waste of time.

I burst from the room, running for the stairs, as visions of my three beautiful sisters, slain and left for dead, infiltrated my head.

'Liana.' I could barely speak, even mentally.

'I'm waiting for you. I will fly faster than you've ever experienced before, and we will check on them.'

She knew. I'd stopped questioning how in my head she was. All the time? Or just when she felt panic and danger? I didn't care right now. We hadn't set the house up with a phone yet. Doing that would register them with the operator system, telling them that my sisters lived there, and Elaine and I agreed we didn't want that, so we'd left it off-grid. I regretted that deeply now.

My thighs burned as I took the stairs three at a time, huffing and puffing.

'Onyx wants to know what's wrong.'

If I told Onyx, he would tell Kohen. I couldn't think of all that right now. I had to think of my sisters.

'Say nothing,' I told her.

When I reached the top of the bunker, a full-on panic had overtaken me. Were they dead? Did that bastard kill my sisters like he'd promised he would? If they were, I would die too. First my mother, then my father—if my sisters were taken from me, I'd have no will to live. I wasn't that strong.

I burst from the door, scaring the guard on duty, and ignored his salute.

Leaping onto Liana's back, I grasped the harness handle, and she shot for the sky. Onyx peered at us with a cocked head.

Did Kohen know and not tell me? If Kohen knew my sisters were going to die and didn't tell me, I'd kill him. I cared for him, but I had limits. Was this why we would stop talking for a long time?

I nearly went mad on the flight to Riverine. I had to close my eyes and tuck my chin to my chest to keep from inhaling bugs. My ears puckered as Liana indeed flew faster than I'd ever seen her before. She was like a rocket.

My heart pounded in my throat as I prepared myself to see my sisters dead. Tears welled in my eyes, and I felt Liana reach out to me with her calming energy.

'Do not count your eggs before they hatch, young one. The bows could have been a threat. If Maxim wants to truly marry you, he knows you won't come willingly if he kills your sisters.'

Her reasoning calmed me a little, but only a little.

'Maybe he doesn't care if I come willingly,' I told her.

'Maybe not. But my sense is that he has some sort of sick obsession with you, in which case he won't want to completely devastate you.'

I'd never wanted some psycho I'd never met before to have a sick obsession with me more than I did at this moment. *Please be secretly in love with me and have kept my sisters alive to please me*, I prayed to the stars.

'He doesn't even know me. Maxim,' I told her.

'Maybe he does. Maybe he's been watching you.'

That thought caused my already wind-chilled skin to chill some more.

I scanned the trees, suddenly wondering if he was watching.

'Liana, you said he had two creatures. What are they?'

I sensed her reluctance at the question.

'Liana, what are they? Did you see them?'

Again, that reluctance washed over me as the wind whipped past so hard my eyes were tearing up.

'You have enough to worry about right now with your sisters, Aisling, I don't want to stress you further.'

That shocked me. She was hiding it.

'I don't care about stress! I have to know what I'm dealing with. What were they, Liana?' This time my voice was firm, and I hoped she could feel the hurt that was rocking through me.

'One was a wolf...' she said, and I relaxed a little. Okay. Like Tetra. Fearsome but not anything to really worry about. *'And the other was a female firebird, like me,'* she said, and all the air whooshed from my lungs.

It was as if she'd knocked every thought from my brain. I couldn't even process her reply. I don't know why I'd assumed she was the only firebird Talanagi. It was vain of me to even think that, but they were rare.

I finally collected my thoughts. *'Do you think Maxim can escape death like me?'*

'We should assume so,' she replied, which caused even more terror to eat away at me.

Another firebird bonded. That changed things.

'Let's deal with one thing at a time,' she told me, and I noticed we were slowing.

Wise words. I wasn't sure I could handle much more. I peered down to see rows and rows of houses come into view.

Riverine.

After a few more moments, I recognized the neighborhood of the house Elaine had bought my sisters to hide them away at.

'Liana?'

'Yes?'

'If Maxim has taken the life of even one of my beautiful sisters, I want you to fly me to Luska so I can kill him. I don't care if he can be reborn three days later. I'll kill again and again and again.'

'Yes, Empress.' There was a loyalty in her tone that caused pride to swell inside of me. She'd do whatever I asked. She had my back.

If he took them, I'd have nothing left to live for. I'd go mad with revenge and tear him limb from limb.

But even as I thought that, one face popped into my mind. He had dark hair, brown skin, and searing blue eyes.

Kohen. *Maybe I'd live for Kohen.*

Those thoughts scared me. It made me vulnerable. Already, I loved too many people. Too many weak points.

Valor, Victory, Virtue, Elaine, Tetra, and now Kohen. Six people I would do anything for.

'Your father was wrong, you know,' Liana said as she landed on the front lawn of our new home. *'Loving isn't a weakness. It keeps you human, so you don't turn into a monster.'*

Was she calling my father a monster?

I didn't care because the second she hit the ground, I burst from her back and ran up the steps of the giant porch, nearly colliding with a guard on duty.

"Empress!" he shouted, looking like I'd just woken him from drowsing on duty. It would be sunrise soon. Another sleepless night.

"Where are my sisters?!" I screamed, sidestepping him.

"They should be—"

I threw open the door, horrified to find it unlocked.

"Val, Vic, Virtue!" I bellowed deep into the house.

There was movement in the back rooms, and I prayed it was one of them. All of them. A shadow passed across the space in advance of their new governess running out from the hallway. She was in sleep clothes, hair a mess, and holding two blades aloft. I had a split second of approval at her warrior-ready stance.

"Are they alive?" I whimpered.

She looked confused, half-lidded eyes with sleep marks on her face. Gwen was in her late twenties, a great pick for the girls' new governess, but I just needed her to speak. Why wasn't she speaking?

"Aisling?" Victory's voice came from behind Gwen, and the governess lowered her swords.

"Empress? What's wrong?" Gwen said, obviously trying to understand why I was there.

"Aisling's home!" Virtue shouted, stumbling out into the hallway next.

My bottom lip shook with relief as tears welled in my eyes.

Where's Val? My heir, the eldest. No, stars, no.

Gwen seemed to finally have gotten her wits about her and had the same thought as me. She spun, kicking in Valor's door while keeping her swords out, and I barreled in after her. Victory and Virtue also caught on that something was wrong and ran into Valor's room after me.

I tore back the blankets, and Valor's eyes snapped open as a scream flew from her throat.

"Aisling, you scared the life out of me!" she said when she recognized me.

I fell on top of her, hugging her tightly as she loosely hugged me back, clearly in shock. A small sob ripped from my throat, and I squeezed her.

"What's going on, Ash?" Victory asked behind me.

I turned, clicking on the light so that I could see them all, appreciating that Gwen still hadn't stowed her blades. She was ready for anything.

"I got a note from... a bad person with a threat to you girls, with this inside." I pulled their three purple bows out, and they all gasped at the same time, which was really eerie.

Victory fingered the bow. "We haven't worn these since your Lottery. They've been missing."

My heart was finally slowing, and Gwen slowly lowered her swords.

"What do you mean? Missing since we moved here or...?" I asked them.

They shook their heads. "Missing since we were at the old house with Father."

Relief washed over me. Maxim must have been watching me for a while, which was an unnerving thought, but he'd probably stolen the bows the night of my father's assassination. Hell, he was probably the one who killed him. Maybe he wanted to hide it because he didn't want me to know, as he was secretly obsessed with me like Liana said?

My father's killer could have been Maxim if he'd been in our home, watching me for weeks, months, if it was since the Lottery.

It meant that, for now, my sisters were safe. But I wasn't taking any second chances.

"I'm scared," Victory said suddenly.

"I'll leave you alone now, Empress," Gwen said. I thanked her, and she left the room.

I climbed into bed with Vic and patted the sheet as the girls slid in next to me.

"I'm glad you're home." Victory yawned, spooning Virtue, who snuggled into her arms. They were feral kittens until they were scared, then they became little marshmallows.

I started to sing a song my mother used to sing when I

was very young, and the girls drifted off to sleep. As I did, I checked in with Liana.

'They're okay,' I told Liana, but I knew that she felt it through our bond.

'They might not be next time,' she told me.

I knew that, too, and I hated that she said it out loud.

'What do I do? Bring them to live on base with me? That's no place to grow up. And they are more likely to get hurt.'

'I agree, but if you leave them here like this, they are sitting ducks.'

'Got any suggestions?' I asked.

'I do. You won't like it, but I think you need to send them into the Wilds to claim a creature early.'

My singing sputtered to a stop.

'Are you insane? They're fourteen! They'll die.'

I glanced down to see Victory fast asleep against me, as was Virtue, but Valor was watching me with wide, fearsome eyes. She said nothing about my stopping the song and just watched me in the pale moonlight that filtered through the window.

'If we train them, they won't. And once they bond creatures and get powers, they will be safer than you could ever make them.'

It was crazy. It had never been done. We went at nineteen—that was the rule.

'You make the rules now. Just think about it.'

I couldn't handle this right now. What Liana was

suggesting was actually ridiculous. Send all three of my heirs into the Wilds at fourteen!

Why was Valor just staring at me like that? Why wasn't she sleeping like the others?

'Because she's most like you. She won't sleep until she's dead tired. She doesn't feel safe. She'd feel safe with a creature watching her back.'

I ignored Liana and reached out to squeeze Val's shoulder. "I'm not going to let anything happen to you," I vowed. "As long as I breathe, you are safe. Do you understand me?"

Valor barely blinked. "What if they kill you, too? Then what?"

Her stark assessment sliced into my heart. She was too young for this.

I sat up. "That's not going to happen."

She sat up too, meeting me head-on. "Father died. He was untouchable. You could be next." Her voice shook.

I had to give her some information to calm her, assurance that I wouldn't die as easily as our father.

"If I tell you a secret, you have to pinky promise you won't tell anyone." I held out my pinky, whispering so I didn't wake the other girls. She hooked her pinky into mine, and I leaned closer.

"I died in the Wilds when I bonded Liana. But because of her power, I was reborn."

Her eyes went wide. "Are you... immortal?" she asked, reverence in her voice.

I shrugged. "I could be. We don't know. But I escaped death once, and I'd do it again just to spare you having to take on too much responsibility while you're so young. I want to give you a normal childhood, Valor."

She frowned. "This is *war*, Aisling. I'm spared nothing. Without peace, I won't ever have a normal childhood. No one will."

There it was again. That word. *Peace.*

Her statement caught me off guard.

In all the years I'd trained for this position, I'd never been taught peace was an option. The war wouldn't end until we conquered Luska and took over their people and lands. Only then would there be true peace.

For a split second I questioned that reasoning, and it felt like my mind fractured. I was warring with everything I'd been taught, and it was such an uncomfortable feeling I just pushed it down, unable to deal with it right now.

"I promise not to die until you're nineteen," I joked, and that got a wry smile out of her. She sighed, looking down at her identical sisters. They looked so peaceful lying there asleep, tangled in each other's arms.

"And I promise that if you do, I'll be a good leader and take care of them," she said.

Tears welled in my eyes at that. She was fourteen. A baby. She shouldn't be thinking like this.

"Do you feel unsafe here?" I asked Valor.

She met my gaze. "I feel unsafe everywhere, Aisling."

It was like a knife to the heart. I realized that my attempt to retain her innocent childhood was fruitless. It had already been broken.

"What would make you feel safer? Do you want to come live with me on base?"

She scrunched her nose up. "Isn't that, like, bombed every day?"

Yes. Dammit.

'Ask her if she wants a creature. If that would make her safe,' Liana prodded.

I swallowed hard, unsure how I felt about that. She could die in the Wilds, and then where would we be?

'She's stronger than you give her credit for,' Liana pushed back at me.

I sighed, hoping I wouldn't regret this. "If you had a bonded creature, would that make you feel safe?"

She sat up fully, her mouth popping open in surprise. "What do you mean? Go into the Wilds early?"

I let out a shaky breath. "I mean, I'm still considering it, but yeah."

She grinned. "Yes, Aisling, that would make me feel safer. With a creature, I could better protect the girls, and while we're sleeping, they could protect us."

She felt unsafe to sleep? I'd been so wrapped up in ruling the country I hadn't really noticed.

"You know, it's Gwen's job to protect you girls."

She shrugged, pulling up the hem of her pajama pants to show me a small dagger stuffed into her sock. "Gwen is great, but I just can't trust anyone to keep us safe anymore."

Wow. She'd grown so much since Father's death. Overnight.

"I need to think about this," I told her. She wouldn't go through the Lottery, which would send a message to the people that I broke the rules. But she was an heir and guaranteed a spot anyway, so maybe it didn't matter. But she wouldn't have an alliance... and she wasn't fully trained yet. I could just be sending her to her death.

'Then train her on weekends,' Liana said.

Valor smiled for the first time in weeks. "Even the fact that you're considering it makes me feel so much better." She leaned forward and pulled me into a hug.

I squeezed her hard, relishing the contact. Valor wasn't a hugger, so this was probably the last one I would get for a while.

When we pulled away, I met her gaze. "While I'm considering this, I want you to train with Gwen during the week, and me on the weekends, on how to survive in the Wilds and how to form a bond and everything."

She nodded eagerly. "I will."

I was exhausted. I'd need a couple hours of sleep before taking on the day, but I wouldn't get it.

"I have to go now, Valor. I am needed back at base."

She frowned but gave me a small nod.

I decided then that the way my father had run our family to think love was a weakness was all wrong. All I'd ever wanted since I became a sister to the triplets was to tell them how much I loved them.

I was empress and leader of this family now, so I was going to start new rules.

I grabbed her chin and forced her to look at me. "Valor Everhart, I love you. And I'm going to start saying that because I want you to know it. I would do anything for you and I will always be here if you need me, no matter what my obligation to this country is. Do you understand me?"

A single tear welled in her eye and spilled over her cheek and onto my thumb.

They weren't alive to hear our mother say I love you; only I had experienced that. So, me saying it was the only exposure she had to the words and how much they could make you feel.

I released her chin.

"It's okay to say those words. Father isn't here anymore, and my new house rule is that love isn't a weakness. It's a blessing. Okay?"

She looked confused but nodded, wiping away her tear. "Okay."

When I left the house, I wondered if I was doing this

right or screwing my sisters up. Parenting was not for the faint of heart.

Now, there was just one more person I needed to say I love you too. Kohen Badshah had my heart fully, and I had to tell him that.

CHAPTER FOURTEEN

I fell asleep on the ride back to base, but it was only a few hours, so I still felt groggy when Liana landed at Sky Reach.

I'd had her tell Onyx that my sisters were safe and to get that message to Elaine before she lost her mind with worry. Even so, Elaine was pacing the courtyard, waiting for me when I returned. Now that it was daylight, I took stock of the base, noting the two huge impact marks that had been made in our south wall and on one of our training fields. But all in all, the buildings were still standing, and repairing the wall and the training field was doable. The base was crawling with soldiers, so I was guessing we suspected the attack was over and it was back to business as normal. I'd have to check in with Commander Ledger about that, but first Elaine...

She ran to me the second I leapt off of Liana.

Her voice shook. "Are they okay?"

I nodded. "They're safe. The bows were taken from my father's house after the Lottery."

She exhaled all of the breath she'd seemingly been holding. Her hair had sprung loose from its bun, and her eyes were rimmed with deep shadows. The only person who possibly loved my sisters more than me was Elaine. She had been with them since they were tiny babies.

"What did the letter say?" I asked her.

Now that I knew my sisters were safe, I was curious about the reply.

She swallowed hard. "It said he will give you three months to reconsider his proposal, at which time he is following through on his promises. And the bows were proof that he can."

"Bastard!" I growled.

Elaine chewed the inside of her lip. "How do we keep the girls safe? Aisling, I think Maxim is capable of the things he says."

Of killing my sisters? Of dragging me against my will to be his wife? Maybe. He had a firebird, too, so maybe.

"Over my dead body. And trust me, I don't die easily," I told her.

She nodded and swallowed hard. "Those girls are everything to me. And I know they are to you, too. So what do we do?"

I sighed, peering at Liana. "Liana thinks I should have

Valor go into the Wilds early and get a creature to help protect her."

Elaine gasped a little and then glanced at Liana with respect. "That might be genius."

"Or it might get her killed," I added.

'Technically, I suggested all three girls go, not just Valor.'

'No way. Val is the only one who might be ready. Trust me.'

Elaine glanced off into the distance as if thinking this through. "Why just Valor? Why not all of them?" It seemed she was having the same thoughts as Liana.

I made a strangled noise in my throat. "They're fourteen! Valor is the only one who would bond strongly right now. The others would have weak bonds, and Victory might not even make it out of a bonding at all."

She'd come out of it with a bunny rabbit or dead.

Elaine swallowed hard. "You're right. But if we could train Val and she could bond strong, I would feel so much better about leaving them in Riverine."

Soldiers passed by us, running to their next destination. I nodded and then stepped closer to my governess, lowering my voice so that only she could hear me. "Until Valor is trained, should we hide the girls away in the country? Take Gwen and a handful of trusted tutors and guards with them? Everyone in Riverine knows what they look like, but in the country..."

Elaine nodded. "They will hate you for it. No friends, no school, or social life..."

I shrugged. "If they are alive to hate me, I can live with that."

"I'll make it happen. Give me your list of trusted people, and I will make sure only they know. Does two months' time seem like enough to get Valor trained?"

I scoffed. "No. But we will have to make it work."

"Just to be clear, in two months we are sending Valor into the Wilds alone to bond early?" Elaine's voice was slightly shaky, as if she, too, were scared of doing such a thing. When it was said so directly like that, fear overtook me.

"Yes," I croaked.

If this Maxim character was as bad as Liana believed him to be, I wanted my sisters to have the best chance at protecting themselves. If I were to die in battle and not be able to become reborn, Valor would have to have a creature before she could rule as empress anyway.

"Are Tetra and everyone still underground?" I asked her. I wasn't about to ask where Kohen was, but that's who I wanted to see.

She shook her head. "They moved to Mohave bunkhouse, topside." She pointed to a maroon brick building in the distance, and I thanked her.

Jogging across the quad, I saluted soldiers as I passed.

When I got to Mohave, I stepped into the women's bunk first. There were half a dozen soldiers inside and just as many creatures lazing about. When they saw me, they all stood at attention, eyes wide as if I was there to inspect their bunks or something. All except Tetra, who stayed lying down and just peered up at me curiously.

"At ease," I told everyone, and they relaxed.

"Hey, Ash," she said, and then she addressed the entire room. "She may be the empress, but she's also my best friend, so she will probably be coming here a lot. You don't need to worry about it."

I grinned at that, and the women in the room seemed to relax a little more.

I sat at the end of Tetra's bed and glanced down at her bad foot. "Are you having a good or bad pain day?" I asked.

"Good. Why?"

"You up for a walk?" I glanced at the other ladies, indicating I wanted privacy, and she nodded.

"Absolutely." She grabbed her cane and hefted herself out of bed as Ariyel popped up from where she had been lying on the floor and looked up at me.

"You can come too," I told her creature, who stuck her snout into my hand to thank me. Again, I was taken aback by the affection from her creature. It meant that in Tetra's mind, we were as good of friends as I thought we were. Sisters, even. It was a relief when I felt I could only trust a handful of people right now.

We went out back and into the woods on a walking path. I was dead tired, hungry, and knew I had a full day ahead of me, but I also needed my best friend to know what had just happened.

I quickly brought her up to speed on Maxim proposing marriage and then the threat to my sisters and the bows.

"They're okay," I pressed when the color drained from her face.

"I just got back from them, but..." I then told her about Elaine's plan to move them to some undisclosed location in the country and Liana's plan to get Valor a creature early.

Her mouth popped open a little at that. "It's scary because it's never been done before that early, but honestly, Aisling, it might be the only way to keep them safe."

"I know." I kicked at some moss on a rock.

"If you asked, my mother would go with the girls as a tutor. She could also help mother them. I worry Valor doesn't have anyone soft around now that you're gone."

"Hey!" I punched her arm. "I'm not soft." It was a sweet offer, though. One I would seriously consider.

She grinned, but then her face took on a serious expression. "You were soft compared to your father, Aisling."

I squirmed at that. She wasn't wrong, but it felt wrong to speak ill of the dead. Why was everyone coming down on my father? Elaine, Caruso, Kohen! Let the man rest in peace.

"He was a widow, a ruler of the country... he did the best he could." Had my mother stayed alive, things might have been different.

Tetra nodded. "I'm just saying, my mom loves your sisters, and if you need someone to help make them feel safe emotionally, I know she would jump at the offer."

Maybe that's what half the problem was. The girls felt like they had no family. Elaine left them to help me. I left them to help the country. They needed a mother figure.

"You know what, T? I'm going to ask her. Thank you."

She gave me a small smile and nodded. "Now, tell me more about Kohen."

I bristled. "What do you mean?"

She gave me that *don't start with me* look, and I burst out laughing.

"Do you think it's obvious to everyone else?"

Tetra shrugged. "Only to me. Or those of us who know you so well. I see the glances you steal across the room. Aisling, you love him."

Hearing her say it cemented it for me. I couldn't help the stupid, goofy grin that graced my face at that moment. "I do."

Tetra was smiling, too, now. "Good for you!" She shook my shoulders. "This is what our youth is for, having forbidden romances with sworn enemies. I live for this."

I raised one eyebrow. "Are you also having a forbidden romance?"

Was her romance with Dev forbidden just because he was Imbrian?

She grinned. "Well, not so forbidden as frowned upon."

That felt wrong. How had we allowed it to come to this division between our peoples? It was so totally wrong, but Imbrians and Amerseans were encouraged to date within their own people only. Had my father started that? Or did it naturally come about within our culture because of the war?

"I should change that," I said.

"Change what?" Tetra asked.

"The *frowned-upon* thing with Imbrians and Amerseans. That's not right. I don't know why we allow it to be. We're one people. We can trust them. It's been over a decade since the Blackout. It's time to show the people that we are happily cohabitating."

Tetra appraised me. "I'm liking this kind of talk. How will you do that?"

"I have no idea. But I'm in charge now, so I'm sure I can figure it out." Maybe being empress wasn't so bad. Maybe I could make a positive difference for the country. I'd always been trained to take over the war, but what if I could fight the prejudice between our people as well? A thrill went through me at the thought. It was as if my father dying had opened my eyes for the first time.

"Kohen is on the training field with Onyx, in case you are wondering." Tetra batted her eyelashes.

I wrapped my arm around her shoulders. "You're amazing. Have I told you that lately?"

She shrugged. "Being your best friend is a tough job, but someone has to do it."

I squeezed her before I let her go and started making my way to the practice field to find Kohen.

As I crossed the main quad, soldiers saluted me left and

right. It was kind of exhausting to have to keep raising my arm to salute them back. Would a head nod do?

"Aisling!" Elaine's voice had me spinning around and chills rising on my arms. It was the tone of her voice that raised the alarm bells. Panic. *What now?* Stars, how much more could I take?

She ran towards me with a large white envelope in her hands. Admiral Caruso and Commander Ledger flanked her.

At the sight of all three of them, I stood taller.

Another letter from Maxim?

"What is it?" I asked.

Commander Ledger took the envelope from Elaine's hands and handed it to me. "The report finally came back on your father's toxicology bloodwork."

I steeled myself, unprepared for this, and yet... excited.

"Does it lead to anything useful?"

"It's classified. For your eyes only." He handed me the envelope, and I turned it over, seeing the red and blue taped seal and tiny printed words.

For Empress Aisling Everhart only.

I peered around me, wondering if I should take this to my office or just open it here. I'd have to speak to Kohen later, I guessed.

"Thank you. I'll go over it and then call a meeting," I told them. I wanted some time alone to deal with whatever it said. If there was somehow evidence in here that pointed to a single person, I wanted to process that alone. Especially since we were looking at fellow Amerseans, someone with close access to my father. Or Maxim. I just didn't know anymore. I didn't want to say it, but it could very well be Caruso who stood before me. Just because she'd been interrogated didn't mean she couldn't lie.

Commander Ledger appeared disappointed by that but saluted me, and then they all left.

'I'm resting in the tree line if you want to open it by me,' Liana offered.

I peered up at the tree line and grinned. *'Are you always stalking me?'*

'I prefer to call it keeping you safe, but yes, I am always looking out for you, Aisling.'

Reading this with Liana felt perfect. I walked across the quad and into the thick forest that blanketed the southern edge of the base.

I found her lazing on the ground with her head nestled in her right wing as she was curled up and nearly asleep.

"I don't want to disturb you," I said as I sat next to her and leaned on her back.

'You're never disturbing me, young one.'

I smiled at the nickname. *'Everyone is younger than you.'*

'True,' she laughed, and it was a cute snorting huff.

I stared at the envelope, my fingers pausing over the seal.

'Are you scared to know who killed your father?'

'Yes,' I answered truthfully. *'What if it's someone I know?'*

'It will likely not state a single person but a toxin that you will have to investigate before finding the actual culprit.'

I knew that. I did. But I also just felt this foreboding feeling in my stomach.

Without overthinking it, I opened the report.

There was a bunch of useless stuff at the top. I scanned right to the conclusion of the report.

> *A new mark was found that only appeared later on the body. It was indicative of a small needle inserted into the neck. Blood toxicology shows a high volume of Hesperus, or "Evening star," an herb found only in the foothills of Imbria. A tasteless, odorless poison.*

It felt like time stopped, and the entire forest tilted on its axis as all the blood rushed to my head.

Foothills of Imbria.

Tasteless, odorless poison.

Meera?

My hands shook as I felt Liana stir under me. I peered at her to find that her eyes were wide.

'Aisling, the needle in the report... remember the blow darts you told me Kohen used on the guards when you both came to free me?'

My eyes flew wide, and my heart stopped beating.

No.

Needle mark.

I won't kiss you again for a long time.

Did Kohen kill my father? Or was he protecting Meera because he knew she did?

Everything I do is to protect you. Remember that.

No...

I stood, heart pounding, hands shaking. My head felt like it was stuffed with cotton. I was so confused.

Liana stood as well, shaking off her feathers, and peered up at me.

'Did Onyx ever say anything—?'

'No. I would tell you.' I could feel the anger rising within Liana. She thought of Onyx as a son. If he hid this from her, she would be livid and devastated.

Maybe I was overreacting. Admiral Caruso interrogated Kohen, and he was found to be clean. So I was back to Meera. Little unassuming Meera.

Folding the papers, I told Liana to be on standby as I walked in a daze to the practice field Kohen was at.

He was alone with Onyx, using some throwing knives on a target stand. As if sensing me coming, he spun, and when I saw his face, my heart sank into my stomach.

Guilt. He looked guilt-ridden.

"No," I said, shaking my head as if that could stop this.

"I had to protect you," he said, and the confirmation caused a sob to rip from my throat.

What was happening?

Kohen had been using me this whole time! He wanted revenge for his father's death, and so he killed mine and spun it as protection.

My devastation quickly turned to rage. My skin began to smoke.

"You killed my father?" I needed to hear him say it. I had to be sure.

"Aisling, listen, your father was behind the attacks on you at school. He wanted you dead—"

"Lies!" I snapped, and a wave of fire flew from me and slammed into him, knocking him back. His eyebrows burned off along with half of his shirt, but his skin was fine. He and I shared the same gift of being impervious to flame.

He looked heartbroken. "I love you, Aisling! But he brainwashed you. He was evil and—"

I exploded with more fire this time, but his own wall of flame flew from his hands and came out to meet mine. The two walls collided, causing a bomb of heat to explode in my face. I didn't care. I was devastated, numb, dead inside.

First Jace, now him. Would men always betray me?

I knew I had to kill him. He'd just admitted to assassinating my father, the emperor. My numbness quickly turned to absolute hatred and rage.

This isn't happening.

Onyx got closer to Kohen, and he slipped his leg over his creature, mounting the black dragon. "Look through his office. You'll find proof of what I'm saying," Kohen begged me as the walls of fire we'd erected between us died out at the same time.

'I need you,' I told Liana. He was going to flee. If he did, I'd use my power on him. I'd control him and force him to stay while I removed him of his head.

"I'm sorry, Aisling," he said, again with the most heartbreaking expression on his face.

Sorry? He'd left my sisters and me orphans, and he was sorry?

It wasn't until Onyx's tail swung out and cracked me in the side of the head that I realized he meant he was sorry for that. Not for killing my father.

I tried to stay conscious, to hold on to reality, but the blow was too hard, and everything went black.

CHAPTER FIFTEEN

I came to with Liana hovering over me and half a dozen soldiers beside her with swords and bows drawn. Their various creatures were scattered across the field, looking all around for a threat.

'Are you okay?' Liana asked.

I had a splitting headache but nodded as all the memories came rushing back to me.

Kohen killed my father!

I stood, swaying a little. *'How long have I been out?'*

There was a siren going off on base and people running around in every direction. The circle of soldiers around me looked ready to fight off a threat.

'Maybe twenty minutes,' she guessed.

I slipped my leg over her back just as Commander Ledger ran up with half a dozen soldiers behind him.

"All the Imbrians have fled the base." He looked at me wide-eyed. "What the hell is going on?"

Of course they did. Anika, Meera, Dev, Kian, they'd all go with him. *The traitor*. The traitor that I almost just said *I love you* to. The traitor who kissed me and told me I'd one day be his wife! What a fool I'd been to fall for that nonsense.

I sat erect on Liana and held my chin up. "Kohen Badshah confessed to killing my father."

I paused for the gasps of the surrounding soldiers.

"I want to lead the fleet into Imbria to get him back and hang him for treason!" I barked.

Commander Ledger's jaw was clenched, his face holding on to barely contained rage.

"Yes, Empress. I'll rally the troops. We will go by train and through the Wilds. He will pay for what he's done."

I nodded. "I'll fly ahead and try to catch him."

"Lieutenant Colt is out on the field, but I'll send him after you when he returns," Ledger offered.

Colt was the only other soldier who could ride on their flying creature.

The crowd of soldiers parted, and then Alek was there, face filled with concern as Iniki flew circles around me, seemingly probing me for wounds.

"Empress, permission to send Iniki with you?" Alek asked, back erect, eyes forward, but I saw emotion stirring there.

Alek, sweet and loyal Alek. Maybe I should have been

looking his way all along—not at the charming poison dripping from Kohen's foul mouth.

"Granted," I said and kicked off the ground, taking for the sky.

Iniki wouldn't be able to keep up with Liana at full speed, but she'd at least be able to trail behind and send word back through Alek. It was helpful.

Liana flew super fast. The wind ripped past me, and I pinched my eyes shut.

'Onyx lied to me,' she said, and there was a jumble of anger mixed with hurt coming off of her. *'I didn't tell you this, but I suspected Kohen right after your father died. I grilled Onyx about it, and he swore Kohen had nothing to do with it.'*

I bristled at that. *'You suspected Kohen?'*

'He's protective of you,' she said.

'Okay, and he was my father. I don't need protection from my own father.'

I sensed something stirring within her, like she wanted to say something to me but then thought better of it. *'Doesn't matter. Kohen shouldn't have killed him. He could have subdued him, locked him away, a hundred other things, and then he lied about it. Kissed you as your heart grieved for the loss of the last parent you had left.'*

Her frank and sympathetic assessment of the situation shook me. Tears bit at the backs of my closed eyes. My throat pinched with emotion as I fought down the sob.

'You can show your feelings to me, Aisling. I won't judge you as weak just because you are human.'

I shook my head. *'Feeling is what got me into this mess in the first place.'* First Jace, then Kohen. I couldn't believe I'd been so naïve.

A deep sadness fell over Liana, filtering through our bond.

'Why are you sad?'

'I'm grieving the loss of a son. Onyx will perish when we kill Kohen.'

I had wondered if she would be okay with that. My killing Kohen, knowing it would hurt Onyx.

Onyx lied to her, but he didn't have a hand in killing my father. Kohen blew the dart into his neck. Kohen planned the whole thing. Onyx was a creature protecting his bonded.

'I'll try to do it in the Wilds if we can catch up with them there before they cross the border. That way, when Kohen dies, Onyx will still be able to breathe.'

'You would do that?' She sounded surprised.

'I don't fault Onyx, not fully.' He had an immature teenager vibe to him. I wasn't even sure how old he was, but I'd avoid killing him if I could.

'Thank you.' I could hear the respect in her voice.

Part of me couldn't believe I was casually thinking about killing Kohen, a man I had just been going to say I love you to. But the other part of me, the part that was raised to be ruthless and not taken advantage of, was ready to cleave his head from his shoulders and light him on fire.

How dare he console me after my father's death and tell me I'd be his wife and kiss me like I was the only woman alive—meanwhile, he harbored this lie.

How fucking dare he!

He was no doubt going back to Imbria to claim his title as king and lead a rebellion against Amersea. I'd been so stupid to entertain the fact that he actually cared for me! I fell right into his trap!

'Stay calm, young one, or you'll explode before we even get there,' Liana advised.

I peered down to see that I was smoking, sending a plume of gray streaking across the sky.

'They are up ahead. I am shielding myself from Onyx. I'll stay back until they hit the Wilds, and then I'll pounce on Onyx from above. He is carrying Anika, Dev, Kian, and Meera as well. I smell them all.'

Of course he was. The bastard. They were all traitors, and if they tried to intervene in justice for my father, I'd kill every single one of them.

'You keep Onyx out of the way, and I'll take care of Kohen,' I told her.

She nodded as she slowed, staying high in the sky, almost in the clouds. The Wilds came into view at the same time the large black dragon did. As Liana gained on them, increasing her speed, my ears popped as she began to descend.

They were lowering, landing in the Wilds!

'What are they doing? They should fly over it and into Imbria,' I said.

Liana was silent for a moment, as if thinking.

'Kohen must have seen this moment. He will be ready. You should be, too.'

She was right. I couldn't discount his gift. I pulled my blade, scanning the trees as Liana lowered over the place they had just been.

When she sank to the ground, I leaped off of her.

'I'm going for Onyx. I smell him near. They split up,' she said.

I nodded, scanning the purple-hued trees. It was ironic that Kohen and I would end where we began. In these very woods, I killed a soldier of my father's Fleet just to save his life. Had I not done that, had I let them end his life, my father would still be here.

A twig snapped behind me, and I spun. Kohen was there, hands out in a gesture of peace, carrying no weapon.

Bad idea.

Kneel, I thought and lashed out with my mind control power before he could try anything.

The silver cord flew towards him, but it bounced off of his chest and hit the ground.

He kept walking towards me, and I backed up in shock. *It didn't work.* My power didn't work on him.

"I have another power I've kept secret from you," he confessed. "Something I only recently discovered."

My heart hammered in my chest. My skin smoked as I built the fire in my chest.

"I am not only impervious to flame, but if I concentrate really hard, I can block other's powers so they don't work on me. Such as Admiral Caruso's."

My mouth dropped open. That was how he'd been able to lie to her.

"And I'm guessing yours, too?" he asked.

I threw my knife quickly, aiming right for his heart, but he dodged it easily, shaking his head. "I've seen this, Aisling." He tapped the side of his skull. "I can't let you hurt my friends because of my actions."

I frowned, pulling my backup blade out. Hurt his friends? My mind wrestled with how to kill him. If I exploded, he was impervious to fire. My mind control didn't work on him. It was going to have to be hand-to-hand combat.

Why was he looking at me like that? Like he adored me? *Sick freak.*

"I'm going to enjoy killing you," I snarled.

He stopped walking, looking crestfallen. "I love you, Aisling. I want you to remember that. I forgive you for what you are about to do to my people."

He was brainwashing me. He had been all along. “Your words mean nothing to me.” I brandished my dagger.

“I just hope you can forgive me for what I have to do now,” he said, and I tensed, my gaze flicking left and right as if expecting an ambush from Anika and the rest of them. “I’ve seen you survive this. Otherwise, I wouldn’t do it.”

My heart raced. I scanned his outstretched hands again, looking for a weapon, for how he was going to kill me.

Then I felt it, at the back of my neck, a prick of pain. I gasped, spinning to see a rustle of leaves behind me before turning back to Kohen. I reached up and yanked the dart out of my neck, but it was already too late. I felt my legs go weak.

I fell to the ground. Kohen lunged forward to catch me, slowly lowering me, and I felt Liana’s energy rip through our bond.

‘Run, Aisling. It’s a trap—’ Then she was no more. Her energy was just... gone.

No. No. No.

How had I been so naïve?

But as I looked up into Kohen’s beautiful face, I knew. Those piercing blue eyes. The bronzed skin. Full lips. Chiseled jaw. I’d been enamored by his beauty and accepted his poison from the second he first opened his mouth to me.

He smoothed my hair. “I would have just put you to sleep, but I need the three days it takes you to rebirth in order to warn my people and get them to safety before you attack.”

The bastard actually had tears welling in his eyes. "You have to search for the truth, Aisling. No one can give it to you, or you won't believe it. You need to know what kind of man your father truly was. Then you will know what I protected you from. When you do, I'll be waiting. I'll *always* be waiting for you. No matter how long it takes, no matter how many bombs you drop on my people, I will always be waiting for you to come back to me." He leaned forward and kissed my forehead. I tried to scream, but only a mumble came out. I couldn't move, and in the center of my chest, a sharp stabbing pain had begun.

Was this how he killed my father?

To kill me in the same way was a double slap in the face.

I'd never hated anyone more than I hated Kohen Badshah.

He'd just provoked war between our peoples, killing the fragile peace we had, and for what? Revenge for his father, the terrorist?

The pain in my chest grew, and a tear fell from his eye and onto my cheek. "Forgive me," he whispered, and then everything went black.

I WAS FLOATING in the serene darkness again with not a care in the world. Nothing to fear and nothing to think about for a long time. I just lay there as if I were in a healing bath.

Slowly, my thoughts returned to me: Kohen's dart in my neck, the poison, and the fact that he killed me. *Bastard!*

Then the golden glowing sun appeared on the horizon, and I felt movement beneath me.

Liana.

She carried me on her back the entire time. My mind grew sharper, and I stood, staring at the sun as it transformed into a beast of fire.

Flames licked across the sky like lightning, and I felt for Liana beneath me, digging into her feathers.

'Be strong. You know what to do,' she said.

I did?

Then she was gone, replaced by clouds, and the fire beast charged at me. I knew then that I'd have to fight the beast like I did last time. This time, I knew it was Liana, and so part of me struggled with the thought of killing it. Did Onyx kill Liana as well? Were we both lying dead in the Wilds?

It didn't matter. It was go-time. I was on my feet as the rushing ball of fire came at me.

My heart beat frantically in my chest. I reached for my sword, only to find it wasn't there.

Last time, I'd had a sword! I should be in battle mode, ready to fight for my life, but instead, all I could keep thinking was how I couldn't believe Kohen killed me.

I've seen myself make love to you under a bed of stars, and I've heard you cry out my name, begging for more.

No matter how much I want to kiss you right now, this isn't where we have our first kiss.

One day, you will beg me to protect you.

This is the last time I kiss you for a long time.

It ends with you as my wife, Aisling.

Every prediction he ever made about us swirled in my head until my heart felt like it would explode.

He lied. He fed me lies until I was putty in his hands. A sob ripped from my throat as the fireball slammed into me, knocking me back. Pain seared along my skin, and I cried out, helplessly batting the fire with my hands.

That did nothing. It consumed me, and I was suddenly trapped in the most horrific pain I'd ever experienced. My skin scorched, peeling as my heart wrestled with Kohen's betrayal.

"Liana, no!" I cried to her. She'd told me once that the fire beast was a part of her. Maybe I could reason with it.

Then I felt her, faint and weak but all around me.

'Use your power.'

My power?

My power!

Of course. Last time, I'd told the fire beast to stop, and it had, and Liana thought it might be because I'd used the thrall.

"Stop!" I cried out, throwing my power wildly around me.

The fire blew outward, but only for a second before consuming me again.

"Stay back!" I cried, and the fire retreated but hovered around me as if it would engulf me at any moment.

I felt the edges of my mind fray as I pushed my power into my command for it to retreat, but the beast kept pushing against me.

It wasn't this hard last time. What was going on? Arms, feathers, and eyeballs could be seen floating in the fire, and I was horrified to recognize one of the eyes as my own.

I knew I had to focus, I knew I had to fight, but the reality was... I was heartbroken. I was barely able to keep my concentration on the beast before me because my mind was with Kohen. My heart was with Kohen.

"Why?" I asked the fire beast. "Why does everyone I love betray me?" I didn't feel like my normal self here. I felt raw and vulnerable and... was I crying? I didn't cry. I wouldn't cry for Kohen!

I screamed in a wild rage and brought my arms down as if they were swords, cutting the beast in half with my mind. It gave a high-pitched shriek and lunged for me again, this time as two halves.

I snapped then. Whatever shred of my humanity remained went feral. I leaped off of the cloud I was standing on and dove for the fire monster. It sandwiched me on both sides, singeing my skin again, but I was ready.

I exploded like a firework at the summer solstice. I lit up

the sky, becoming one with the fire beast. I became fire, fighting the beast with its own medicine. I burned through it, getting hotter and bigger, until the entire sky was on fire.

I was filled with so much rage that even death couldn't hold me. I knew then that I had to live so that I could go back and kill Kohen. It was now my greatest mission to see him beg for his life and admit that everything he said to me was a lie.

The last thing I remembered before my fire consumed the beast was screaming into the sky as my heart wept.

I vowed then and there to never love again. Not for as long as I lived, even if that was forever.

CHAPTER SIXTEEN

A voice said: "Her vitals are good. Skin is pink, but no more burns. She's healing nicely."

I felt like I was stuck under a hundred-pound blanket, trying to pull myself up out of a dream.

"Let me know when she wakes." Elaine's voice gave me the boost I needed to fully open my eyelids.

"Tell her yourself," said an elderly male doctor wearing a white coat—the voice I had heard. He saluted me.

"Aisling!" Elaine threw herself over me, pulling me to her chest.

I was in a large medical room with the privacy curtains pulled shut and bright lights shining in my face. I tried to say something back to her, but my voice was a croak. My tongue stuck to the roof of my mouth.

"Let me examine her quickly, then I can give you privacy," the doctor said.

Elaine stepped away from me, worry in her gaze. The doctor, who had a head of thinning silver hair, was barely holding on to a grin as he handed me a glass of water and helped me sit up.

"Immortality? Empress, it's... amazing. You're... *amazing*." He sounded starry-eyed, and I wasn't in the mood for it. How many people knew I could rebirth? Where was Kohen? How long had I been out?

"Liana?" I suddenly remembered my creature.

'I'm outside waiting for you. Glad you made it, young one.'

"She's fine—right outside," Elaine told me.

The doctor held a stethoscope to my chest, and I batted him off. "I'm fine. You're dismissed."

He frowned. "Empress, I don't think that's wise—"

"You're dismissed," I said again, this time more harshly.

He swallowed hard, nodding, and left the room.

Elaine released a shaky breath and opened her mouth to speak, but I cut her off.

"How long have I been out? Did you find Kohen?"

"Three days. And no. But we've sent in a heavy contingent of soldiers looking for him. They've... met resistance, though."

I barked out a laugh, standing slowly and gripping the corner of the bed rail as Elaine rushed to my side.

"Of course they have. Kohen killed my father, then he killed me, and now he's trying to take back his country."

Elaine growled. "Well then, we burn it to the ground."

I nodded, glad she was thinking along the same lines as me. She helped me out of my gown and into clean clothes.

"Iniki found both you and Liana dead in the wilds. Creatures were circling your body. She held them off until we could get there."

I'd have to thank Alek. Waking up from being reborn only to die again would have sucked. I wasn't sure how many times I could fight that fire beast. It seemed stronger this time.

Elaine dragged a finger across my arm and the light pink skin there. It looked like I had a sunburn.

"Your entire skin was charred, Aisling. You looked—" Her voice caught. "But Tetra forced us to keep you in here. Said you would be... reborn. I wasn't really sure what happened last time. We never talked about it in detail—" She was mumbling, and I placed my hands on her shoulders to steady her.

"I'm okay. You did everything right," I told her.

Her mouth set into a grim line. "Aisling, I've raised you since you were little. You're like a daughter to me. Seeing you... dead like that... was—" She stared off into space. "I never want to go through that again, but is this something that might happen again? Are you really immortal?"

'Am I immortal?' I asked Liana. *'Will I age and grow old?'* I suddenly wondered.

'You will grow old, yes. And you are immortal so long as you can fight the fire beast. One day, when you are old and gray, you may no longer be able to fight her, and then you will join your place among the stars.'

Okay, that was a lot to process. "Kind of," I told Elaine.

She blew air out through her teeth. "Too many people saw. We couldn't keep this secret. They are chanting *immortal empress* in the streets. The people have been inspired by this. They think you will reign forever and be able to protect them against anything."

My stomach dropped. That was a lot of pressure.

"Immortal empress? Maybe that's a good thing. Maybe that will make its way back to Maxim and Imbria."

Elaine nodded. "It could be a good thing."

I rolled out my neck, readying myself for what was ahead. "Okay, it's time to declare war on Imbria. If they are trying to separate, we have to shut it down before Kohen can take control." I moved to the door, and Elaine stepped out in front of me to slow my progress.

"Aisling, there is one more matter to discuss first," she said, chewing her lip.

I braced myself because she looked like she was about to deliver unsettling news.

"Some rumors have started here at the base. Jace was

overheard telling people that you kissed Kohen at the graduation ball—"

"Jace ratted me out!" I screamed.

I never should have publicly kissed Kohen. That was so stupid. I never should have kissed Kohen at all. But at the time, my father was still alive, and I hadn't known I'd be empress a day later.

"Yes," Elaine said. "And so now people see that Kohen wormed his way into your heart and then killed your father and you. They think your decision-making is..."

I glared at her. "What?"

"Weak. The admirals are calling for you to get engaged now and then married within a year, someone loyal to the empire."

"Oh, because as a woman, I'm weak and fragile, and I need a man to help me think?" I snapped and then realized it wasn't Elaine's fault. She was just delivering the news.

Take a husband? I knew that would come eventually, but so soon?

"I'm sorry," I told Elaine. "This is just a lot."

She nodded, giving me a compassionate look. "Aisling, we always knew you would be empress one day and take a husband and have heirs."

She was right. "Do you think my decision-making is weak?" I asked her.

She paused for too long, and my mouth popped open as hurt crept into my heart.

"Hang on, let me explain." She reached out and grabbed my hand.

"I think choosing to trust Kohen Badshah enough to let him into your heart was stupid. I will not mince my words on that," she declared.

There was the Elaine I knew and loved my entire life.

"But," she went on, "I trust that every decision you make is for the good of the empire, and one mistake will not blemish your reign over this country. We just need to fix this now so it can move to the back of people's minds."

I sighed. "Okay."

She nodded. "Okay. Your friends are outside. You should see them quickly and then meet me in the war room with the admirals to choose your husband."

"*Then* we can go to war against Imbria?" I pressed her.

She nodded. "Then we are all prepared to follow your lead on that."

Okay, that was good. It sounded like an ultimatum, which I didn't like, but my father had taught me that keeping the admirals and those high up in the chain of command happy and making them feel heard was important. I was going to get married sooner or later. Better that my people saw I would marry for the good of our country. Especially before this rumor of my being intimate with Kohen got out.

Kohen. I was still in shock at everything that had happened with him.

Why move aside on the first day to allow Tetra to stand near me at the Lottery?

Why leave his alliance so that I would take over and protect his friends when he could have done that?

Why protect my life when I was attacked at school?

Why help me get Liana right after we'd bonded and the Luskins had taken her?

Why, why, why? I had more questions than answers, but it really was simple when I took my heart out of the equation. He did all of that, so I would trust him. With that trust, he got close to my father and killed him. And now he was back in Imbria with his friends, probably working with a rebel faction to become king again and break away from Amersea.

We'd be two nations again, and I'd be fighting two wars, one with Luska and one with Imbria. No, I wouldn't let that happen.

"Aisling?" Elaine peered at me and I cleared my throat, slightly embarrassed about being lost in my thoughts.

We stepped out of the medical center, and when we got outside, Tetra threw herself at me.

"That rat bastard!" she growled.

She was talking about Kohen. If I had my way, I'd never hear his name again.

"I'm so glad you're okay." She squeezed me so tightly it hurt, but I squeezed her back.

When we pulled away, I noticed Alek and Roc were

standing with her, concern etched across both of their faces. Their creatures hung back a few feet behind them—except for Iniki, who was perched on Alek's shoulder.

I looked at her and Alek. "Thank you for your help."

Alek nodded, frowning. "Of course. I'm glad to see you alive... again."

The unsaid thing hung in the air like a pungent perfume.

I died and came back to life.

It was weird. I should probably address it, but I didn't have the energy right now.

Roc saluted me. "Permission to be on the front lines when we dish out payback to Kohen and Imbria."

I grinned. "Permission granted."

Roc was loyal, always had been.

Tetra peered at the boys. "Can I speak to her alone, please?"

They nodded, and Alek gave me one last lingering look before they walked away.

When I was finally facing just my bestie, I felt some of the cement wall around my heart crumble.

"Ash." She placed her hands on my shoulders. "I know how much you cared for him. I'm so sorry. I feel partly at fault for encouraging you to like him."

I shook my head. "You didn't do this, Tetra. He was calculating from the second he saw me on Lottery Day. This was always his plan. Anika and the others, too."

I knew she'd grown close with Anika.

She chewed her lip, and I saw something cross her face.

"What?" I asked her, eyeing the door to the war room behind her. I was expected there soon.

"I was with Anika when it all went down. Kohen showed up and just gave her a nod. Then she grabbed my shoulders and said some crazy stuff."

I pursed my lips. "Like what?"

She shook her head. "It's crazy, Aisling. Can't be true."

"Like what?" I pushed.

She chewed her lip, like even saying it would get her in trouble. "She said your dad was the terrorist, not Kohen's. That he was behind the attacks on your life at school and the attack on the train station during the Blackout."

I barked out in laughter, and Tetra seemed to relax.

"I know. It's too wild to be believable," she agreed.

I nodded. "And what an easy scapegoat for them to explain their behavior." My father bombing his own people and trying to kill his own daughter? It was asinine. But for a split second, a darker part of me wondered if he would do such a thing? *No*. Kohen had put that in my head, and if I went down that path, he won.

"Doesn't matter." Tetra waved me off. "It was crazy, and I'm in shock. I can't believe they all lied to us like that. I trusted them."

"Me too. Every single one." Even little Meera who blow-darted my neck!

She pulled me in for another hug. "I'm here if you want to talk," she whispered in my ear, and I nodded.

Lastly, I walked over to Liana. She'd been waiting patiently off to the side for me. I wrapped my arms around her neck and snuggled into her feathers, letting her calming energy wash over me.

'Kohen killed me,' I told her. Technically, it was probably Meera, but I knew she did nothing without his command.

'Onyx took my life, too.' I could hear the hurt in her voice.

'They have to pay,' I warned her. I would eventually find Kohen and kill him, and Onyx would die as a result of that.

'I know that,' she said, but there was something else there, too. Confusion?

I pulled back and met her gaze.

"What?" I asked. I'd known her long enough now to know when something was bothering her.

'What Anika told Tetra lines up with what Onyx told me,' she mused.

'So what? They have all corroborated their insane story? It means nothing.'

'Maybe,' she said.

I growled, taking a step back from her. *'I don't have time for this. The admirals want me to choose a husband, and I'm about to declare war on Imbria. I need to know you are with me one hundred percent.'*

She bowed until her beak touched my feet. *'I am yours to command, Empress.'*

Pride swelled in my chest at her loyalty. A loyalty I wasn't sure I deserved.

'Thank you.' I petted her neck feathers as she raised her head, and then I made my way to the war room.

I hated that being a woman not tied to a man made me look weak. At this point, I'd be fine never getting married or having children and just letting the triplets have families of heirs and take over when I was too old. Between Kohen and Jace, I was done with love. This would be a marriage of convenience. No love involved. So, I just wanted to get it over with.

CHAPTER SEVENTEEN

When I entered the room, it was pandemonium, people running every which way, talking on radios and drawing on maps.

"What's going on?" I asked.

Commander Ledger was speaking to Lieutenant Colt. When he saw me, he broke away and approached me. "Imbria has declared sovereignty. They state that Kohen Badshah is their new king."

"They're separating?" I growled.

That bastard. I knew it. He used me. I wanted to scream, to punch my fist through a wall. But I just stood there.

Ledger nodded. "Amerseans in the area have been marched to the border and told to evacuate. They are setting up a temporary wall."

"A wall? It's our land!" I screamed, and half a dozen people turned to look at me.

"Not anymore," the commander whispered. "Not unless you want to take it back by force."

"Of course I do," I told him. "We're not giving up half our country."

Imbria and Amersea had been one for nearly all my life. Splitting again, different rulers, different territories... it wasn't happening. My father would roll over in his grave. That bastard Kohen had planned this all along!

My mind went back to the people on the border of the Wilds that I'd met in the small city, to Kohen's brothers in Sorak, and I faltered. "I don't want civilian casualties, okay? I just want Kohen."

Ledger frowned, his brows bunching together on his forehead. "Casualties are a byproduct of war, Empress. I can't give you Kohen without death and destruction."

My stomach tightened into knots. Why did I feel like this was wrong? Kohen snuck into my heart and murdered my father before killing me. Then he'd taken half of *my* country. I was well within my right to fight back.

"Empress, I need permission to green-light this mission," the commander said.

I took in a deep breath. "Burn their half of the Wilds *and* their military bases. Leave the cities alone for now."

He nodded and left, and it felt like a knife had twisted in my chest.

Then I remembered something he'd said: *You attack Imbria first, Aisling. You lead an angry mob of soldiers into our land, and you burn a lot of it down.*

Was that what this was? The fulfillment of one of his prophecies? Or was he controlling my actions with his predictions? And now I was doing them because he made me think I had no choice?

I wanted to bash my head against the wall in an effort to clear my thoughts.

"One more thing." Commander Ledger slid a piece of paper in front of me and handed me a pen. "The admirals and I have made a list of top candidates to be your husband. This will make the entire empire look strong, so we are eager for your choice."

I hadn't looked down at the list yet. "I can only choose from this list?"

His face was cold as steel. "That is advisable, Empress."

A veiled threat.

With that, I peered at the list and actually laughed out loud at the first name.

Jace Ledger.

I crossed it out right in front of the commander. "Hell no," I said out loud and didn't bother looking up to see his reaction.

Roc Keerin
Tyson Buckley
Tucker Corry
Calvin Bolton
Alek Warden

Six men. Only six men in the entire country were good enough to be my husband in the eyes of the admirals?

I hovered my pen over one name, wondering if it would be a mistake. The number of people I could trust was slowly drying up, and this person was about the only one on this list I thought I might be able to sleep next to without wanting a knife under my pillow.

I circled Alek's name and handed it back.

The commander nodded. "I'll inform him. We can spread the word about the engagement throughout the country. It will boost morale."

Oh joy.

An engagement right before declaring war because a single woman was weak. Just what I always wanted.

I didn't care at this point. I'd marry Jace if it meant the admirals would approve my plot for revenge. Kohen Badshah would pay for what he did to my family. I wouldn't stop until his head was on a spike in the middle of Emberlane Park for all to see.

'Don't let this change who you are, Aisling,' Liana warned.

'Too late,' I told her, and for the first time, I shut down our bond, closing off my connection to her.

I was dead inside. Kohen had killed whatever shred of lovable me was left. I was choking on the lies he had gagged me with.

The End.

Book three, *Lies that Blemish*, can be preordered on Amazon. Check LeiaStone.com for the latest news.

About Leia Stone

Leia Stone is the USA Today bestselling author of multiple bestselling series including Matefinder and Wolf Girl. She's sold over three million books and her Fallen Academy series has been optioned for film. Her novels have been translated into multiple languages and she even dabbles in script writing.

Leia writes urban fantasy and paranormal romance with sassy kick-butt heroines and irresistible love interests. She lives in Spokane, WA with her husband and two children.

www.LeiaStone.com

JOIN THE FAN CLUB

Get involved, make some friends, and get exclusive sneak peeks before anyone else.

News:

Also join my Newsletter! (Link on my website Leias tone.com) I only send one out when I have a new release or something exciting.

Shop:

Shop in my store! (LeiaStoneBooks.Com) I have special editions and ebook bundles and more!

 *Leia*

BOOKS BY LEIA STONE

SEE FULL LIST AT LEIASTONE.COM/BOOKS

FANTASY

Vampire Hunter Society

Shifter Island Series

Wolf Girl Series

Daughter of Light Series

The Titan's Saga

Supernatural Bounty Hunter Series

Dream Wars Series

Fallen Academy Series

Dragons & Druids Series

Matefinder Series

Matefinder: Next Generation

Hive Trilogy

NYC Mecca Series

Night War Saga

Water Realm Series

The Kings of Avalier Series

Gilded City Series

ACKNOWLEDGMENTS

This has been one of my favorite series to write! A special thank you to my husband who is from India and is my inspiration for Kohen 🤍 A huge thank you to my editor Lee and my proofer Brit for polishing this baby up! I'm so grateful to my Wolf Pack and ARC team and ALL my readers for supporting me over the years. Thanks to my kiddos for sharing mommy with her characters and Thank you to God for giving me this amazing creative gift.

www.ingramcontent.com/pod-product-compliance
Lightning Source LLC
Chambersburg PA
CBHW020459310726
48979CB00016B/2728/J

* 9 7 8 1 9 5 1 5 7 8 4 7 3 *